P9-BEE-223

WITHDRAWN

EX LIBRIS

SOUTH ORANGE
PUBLIC LIBRARY
WITHDRAWN

SQUANDERING THE BLUE

ALSO BY KATE BRAVERMAN

Fiction

Lithium for Medea

Palm Latitudes

Poetry

Milk Run

Lullaby for Sinners

Hurricane Warnings

Postcard from August

SQUANDERING the BLUE

stories

KATE BRAVERMAN

FAWCETT COLUMBINE ▪ NEW YORK

BRA
✓

A Fawcett Columbine Book
Published by Ballantine Books
Copyright © 1989, 1990 by Kate Braverman

All rights reserved under International and
Pan-American Copyright Conventions. Published in
the United States by Ballantine Books, a division of
Random House, Inc., New York, and simultaneously in
Canada by Random House of Canada Limited, Toronto.

Stories in this collection have appeared in *The Los Angeles Times Magazine*,
Lear's, *American Voice*, *Crosscurrents*, and *Story*.

Library of Congress Cataloging-in-Publication Data
Braverman, Kate.
Squandering the blue, stories / Kate Braverman.—1st ed.
p.   cm.
ISBN 0-449-90551-9
I. Title.   II. Title: Squandering the blue.
PS3552.R3555S68   1990
813'.54—dc20   90-34694
                                                  CIP

Manufactured in the United States of America
Designed by Beth Tondreau Design/Jane Treuhaft
First Edition: October 1990
10   9   8   7   6   5   4   3   2   1

For my students,

the Brentwood Ladies,

and the women of the rooms.

CONTENTS

SQUANDERING

THE BLUE

I T WAS IN MY SIXTH YEAR, SHORTLY BE-
fore my birthday, that my mother took us to live with her
mother, Dominique, in Beverly Hills. In my perception, we
were one moment walking along the beach in Maui, the
sky an intoxication above us, and the next, we were beside
my grandmother's swimming pool, the calm water blue and
alluring. I did not recognize that we had crossed a border
between worlds. It seemed we were merely located in a
somewhat different region of a perpetually warm and luminescent continuum.

I was immediately enrolled at Westford Academy. I wel-
comed the sense of ritual, the order, the uniforms and
schedule. When I climbed the steps of the school bus on
my first day, I had the sensation that my life, at last, was
beginning. I was not frightened. I did not look back.

My mother was a poet. She had educated me in an eccentric mode of her own design. In Mexico, where I was

born and lived until I was three, I had a local girl as a nanny. I have seen pictures of this house perched on a cliff above an ocean implausibly blue. It was in this house that my mother finished her fourth book of poetry, *Squandering the Blue*, a manuscript ultimately published by a now long-bankrupt small press. Not a single copy still exists.

The house itself survives in photographs. It was in this small white villa washed by a constant salt wind that my mother stared at the sea below, finding a vast and remote blue space within herself, some intimation of a profound necessity that she forced into stanzas while I learned to speak Spanish. What I learned at three I would forget immediately, though I suspect there is somewhere within me a certain capacity for a kind of blue, a sea rhythm, perhaps, salt air or waves.

After Mexico, my mother took us to Kyoto where she taught for one year at the university, studied Zen, and wrote the poems that would later be published by a small press in Oregon as *Green Tea at Dawn*. I have found one review of this book which called the poems too still and private, too meditative, lacking the flamboyant sense of the dramatic that her earlier work had possessed.

"When my ship comes in, I'll be too weak to meet it," I remember my mother saying, lighting a cigarette and laughing.

The sound of typewriter keys informs my recollection of Japan. The sound of the typewriter and falling rain and a sense of cold in the air. In Kyoto, I was four and educated solely by my mother. She read poetry to me in the garden.

It was after Japan, when her trust fund was almost entirely exhausted, that we lived in the jungle of Maui. I cannot find a line between my actual memories and the reconstructions I have been able to make, reinventions based largely on my mother's Maui poems. It has become part of my personal history, those disputable facts and their shifting resonances that we all carry and somehow both believe and doubt, to think my schooling consisted of walking with my mother from our shack beside a river to a similar dwelling where children were communally taught the alphabet and counting every other morning, weather permitting.

I am certain of nothing before Beverly Hills. Still, an image asserts itself aggressively at the periphery. I seem to want to remember my mother at night, opening a suitcase and packing, agitated. She would have done this by flashlight and lantern. We had no electricity in the jungle. There would have been the smoky shadows I took as the unquestionable face of the night. My mother finds an old pair of high heels that she has not worn in years. She puts them on and walks with effort through the one room of our wood and chicken-wire shack on a river of red ginger in the jungle. My mother, stumbling and laughing and not alone. Night with the smell of kerosene and what I later learn is marijuana. My night is fragmentary, seen through mosquito netting. But I must be imagining this. If she was packing anything in this partial memory, it would be notebooks and pages of manuscripts. I have heard Dominique say, at a cocktail party or over the telephone, that we crawled out of the jungle with only the clothes on our back.

Then the green arms of Beverly Hills, a crisp and ordered green after the dense excess of the jungle pulled us in. There was the sense of something assured and dependable, like the cradle I already suspected I did not adequately have. I am talking with my grandmother on the brick terrace near the green tile swimming pool. The gardener is cutting and mowing. I am swimming with Dominique. I do not see my mother. She does not like to swim, she does not like the sun. Dominique and I are tanned, glistening with chlorine

like beads on our skin. My mother chooses to be remote,
on the edge of the yard, in shade. She is staring at the bird
of paradise poking orange and purple between bougainvillea. She is erased of expression. There is a notebook on her
lap, a pen in her hand, but she writes nothing. The pages
are blank. I sense there is a disturbance in this abundance
of white. I am somehow afraid I will be blamed for this,
but I am not.

It occurs to me that I am half expecting punishment for
my mother's inability to write because I have somehow
willed this for her, this severing from her source, this exile
and erasure. I do not like her relentless chicken scratches
and her refusal to swim and sunbathe, to laugh and tan as
we do. My mother embraces the periphery and I will her
to fade completely.

This is a land of magic. She complies. She becomes part
of the background, like the water sprinklers, the gardener,
the maid. I barely think of her. My world is now dense with
fences and anchors, the routine and predictable. I like this.
Somehow I sense that there will be no more nights lit by
candles and the sound of long-haired men playing guitars.
My mother will not laugh anymore in a night smoky from
cigarettes and kerosene, in a night punctuated by rain. All
of this has been banished.

I wear gray-and-white uniforms to school. This does not
vary. The school bus arrives precisely at eight, without fail.
Even the climate has been revised. It is always warm and
rainless. And what my grandmother says to my mother
never alters. It is a perpetual quiet litany of how my mother
has failed. My mother should do something with her edu-
cation, like teach English. My mother should get married.
Her hair is a scandal. She drinks too much. Dominique and
I share glances. We know how to float on rafts in the pool
in the hot afternoon. We know how to make the sun love

our skin. We are agile and strong. Dominique and I are conspirators, nodding in perfect agreement.

One day, I realize with absolute clarity that I am different. It is at a school festival, the May fair or the Halloween party. I suddenly recognize that, simultaneously, I have no father and my mother has no husband. Everywhere, my classmates are clustered in groups of three or four or five. My mother and I are glaringly, flagrantly it seems to me, the exception. We are only two. I am breathless with rage. My mother has burdened me with her defects, her terrible flaws. I am conscious of this then, at that moment, and later, when I must say that my parents are divorced. I feel humiliation and shame.

There is a further level in this first intimation: my mother and I are only two. I recognize that this, like the blank pages in my mother's notebooks, is an unacceptable absence. I am afraid that this lack is being noticed and remarked upon by others. I suspect that I am also to blame. I am not blamed. Somehow, I believe that Dominique will not permit this.

I cannot determine years with any certainty. There are images that seem identical in their dimension and intent, though surely I am older now. I am at the house of a classmate. I am adroit with people, always. I am surrounded by friends. I am standing in a child's playhouse set in a backyard beyond the swimming pool and tennis court, in a part of the yard where the ground refuses the insistent demand of order and swells with the unruly and the tropical. A part of the backyard that asserts the premise of the indigenous, a place where the ground refuses to be manicured. There is a bird's nest, perhaps, and vines with mice, hedges of red-and-yellow hibiscus thrashed by latania.

I am playing tea party with Ashley or Courtney or Chelsea. It is my idea. It is always my idea. I get to be the mother.

I am placing teacups with pink roses painted on their sides in matching saucers. I am arranging plates on a flowered cloth and I sense my mother approaching. I do not hear her. It is rather that I become aware of her nearness as one might sense the ocean or a storm before you see it. There is an alteration in my personal climate. I look out the miniature window of the playhouse, the window with small white lace curtains, and she is approaching.

Invariably, my mother is navigating the green expanse of the grounds, the irregular green path between lawn and grass as if she were walking on a ship, unsteady, with enormous effort. Her chin is set, tense. She is walking as if her life depended on it.

I am on a tennis court, and certainly I am older. Suddenly I am completely blinded by sun. It is not the sunlight which is, without warning, disorienting me but rather the subliminal agitation I experience when my mother is near. I am shading my eyes and still I am unable to return a simple shot. She is coming toward me, walking unbalanced, as if the gravity of this world took her by surprise. Her hair is too long. She has stopped dyeing it. Her hair is partially gray. It looks dirty. And she is wearing blue jeans and sandals. I can't stand her. The other mothers wear nylons and skirts and high heels, even when they have been in skiing accidents and have limbs which are bandaged. I think my mother is the perpetual victim of an accident without a name; her damage is permanent. I am without fail embarrassed. I avoid contact with her eyes. Always, her eyes register with something I am later to identify as wonder, contempt, and terror but misread, as a child, as merely something deeply startled.

It is that startled quality, the wide and too full eyes that informs my childhood. It is her startled eyes and how she stumbled as she walked, as if the ground were somehow denser and more complicated than she had expected. I do not remember when my discomfort hardened and I became bitterly ashamed of her. Perhaps it was shortly after my eighth birthday, my second birthday in Beverly Hills, when my mother began attending meetings.

I did not feel relief when my mother joined Alcoholics Anonymous. Rather, I felt a kind of scorn. The beast which had no name now had a history, a morphology. There was a category for my mother, after all. It seemed to make her smaller. AA seemed to me the stuttering beginning of an alphabet I did not expect her to master. How could she? She could barely comb her hair and walk. She sat in the shade. She couldn't even soil pages with the words no one wanted.

In the distance, I am aware of my mother suddenly animated and often absent in the evenings. She is going to meetings. Dominique and I exchange glances which say this will not last. She has no grace. She is a creature of the rudiments. She cannot even find a decent hairdresser. She cannot recover.

There are moments when my mother occupies my attention. I am angry when she intrudes, when she does not erase herself. The telephone is ringing constantly. She is driving others to meetings. She is promoted and now entrusted to make coffee, sweep floors, and bring cookies. The kitchen smells of her chocolate chip cookies. The kitchen cabinets are stocked with bags of chocolate chips, canisters of flour and sugar, tins of cinnamon.

I would enter the kitchen in the morning, dressed in the uniform which reassured me, and find my mother standing near the oven, wearing a bathrobe, distracted, chain-smoking. Trays of chocolate chip cookies would be cooling on the tile counter. My mother often baked cookies all night, usually immediately before the temptation to drink became irresistible. Then for weeks or months there would be no cookies. My mother would be drinking, the door to her room locked, a bottle of vodka on the night table. The radio would be playing the Rolling Stones or the Eagles.

Then, suddenly, the trays of cookies and stacks of cookies in aluminum foil would reappear. She was attending meetings and doing the first three steps. She was admitting that her life was unmanageable. She was praying that a power greater than herself would restore her to sanity. And she was struggling with the third step, the step which required that she turn her will and her life over to the care of God as she understood him. The problem was that my mother did not understand God.

My mother remains out of focus in these memories. It is as if the cycles of disease and remission, the waves of abstinence, temptation, and obsession that comprised her life, run through my recollections, blurring her anxious face, pale even in the California summers, like a photograph of someone moving too fast.

There was something I now see as achingly intangible and unsustaining, even in her successes. The Maui poems, finally published by a feminist press in New Mexico, did not seem to matter in Beverly Hills. The fathers of my classmates won Academy Awards. Photographs of their mothers appeared in fashion magazines. Was there a triumph in a slender volume available only by special order from an obscure press in a distant state? I thought her poems were a dubious enterprise, an excuse for failing to live normally. Dominique said it was a form of therapy. Then she would say it was vulgar and cheap. I did not disagree.

Ask me what I felt when I saw the book was dedicated to me. I felt a desire to run from the room. I did not want my name on the front page. I did not want to be publicly associated with her. I did not want to pretend to be pleased.

And why do I seem to remember that my mother placed the book on my bedroom table, later, when it was dark? Can it be that I simply stood there and my arm refused to move, to reach out, to take what she was offering?

I recall vividly a summer when my mother seemed to possess a rare sense of purpose. She sat in the shade of the terrace, at a glass-surfaced table cluttered with papers, books, dictionaries, packages of cigarettes, ashtrays, and soda bottles. She was translating from the Spanish love poems written by women. Four months later the editor would change his mind and decline to publish the book. My mother walked from the mailbox with the cancellation letter to the liquor cabinet. I am standing in a bathing suit. She is unscrewing the cap from a bottle. She is studying the side of the bottle.

"It's the labels," she is musing, "enticing as a postcard from Kauai. Or a medieval script, an illumination imposed upon the pagan."

I seem to remember her saying this, though I might have invented these particular words. In this memory, my mother looks directly at me. She says, "Understand. I have prayed for humility. I have prayed for surrender. I have tried to comprehend God. And this"—she is holding the cancellation letter and the bottle at the same time—"is God's answer. Perhaps I'll answer my own prayers." Then she is pouring vodka into a glass. But of course I cannot actually remember this, I must be reconstructing this dialogue from some intangible evidence, like a shadow not on the lungs but on the soul.

I feel distant and superior. The cancellation letter my mother holds proves that she is deficient and suspect. Of course they will reject her. The implication is that she deserves this. I cannot tell her I love her. I must deprecate her, must push her into a safe and resolved distance. The idea of wrapping my wet body around her, of pressing my chlorine draped flesh into hers does not occur to me. I do not say this rejection is unfair, the project worthy, the translation excellent, and no, you must not drink, must not take even the first sip.

Whatever my mother knows is obscure and intrinsically flawed. I have all the evidence. She cannot provide me with a father. She doesn't make any money. No one has ever heard of her. We have to live with my grandmother. And Dominique can't stand her. My mother can't even stay sober. The other mothers play tennis and bridge, they make dinner parties, attend premiers, and go on location. They are tanned and assured. They don't have gray hair. My mother is not like them at all. I don't care if she drinks vodka until she dies.

I am eleven years old. It is summer. We have lived in Beverly Hills for nearly five years. My mother is not drinking. She is not absorbed in anything now that would make her remote. Her bedroom is no longer locked. There is something airy and green, a sense of the lavish in this summer. My mother joins me in the pool. I am astonished that my mother can wear a two-piece bathing suit and swim. Some border has been crossed. Time seems to elongate.

It is late in the afternoon. I have been swimming with my mother. I have followed her to her bedroom. I am looking through the doorway to her green tile bathroom. She is taking a bath with her bathing suit still on. It suddenly occurs to me that this behavior is unacceptable. I realize that I have seen this particular repetition for an unnaturally long period of time. I, who pride myself on my immunity to her moods and eccentric expressions, am forced to ask why she is bathing with her swimsuit on.

"There is something I choose not to see," my mother said, as if that explained everything.

Then it is a bit later, perhaps August. We, Dominique and I, know that she has breast cancer. We know she has concealed the lump on her breast for months or even years. That is why she wears her bathing suit in the bathtub. The lump is the size of an egg. The tumor in her breast is inoperable.

My mother is baking chocolate chip cookies and listening to the radio. It is Bob Seger or Jackson Browne. She knows the words. She sings. She is sober and I realize that she has been for over a year. She refuses painkillers. She is extraordinarily pale. She is smoking a cigarette. "I prayed and God answered." She smiled. "This pain"—she pauses, cannot describe it—"this is an answer I can understand. I have finally found a sobriety I can comprehend."

I am swimming laps, twenty, thirty, forty. I am afraid to stop. If I stop swimming, I will be sucked down to the center of an expanse I cannot bear to imagine. She is on the far side of the pool, watching me, her face so entirely illuminated with emotion that I do not dare look at her.

"I am completely surrendered," she says with a sense of wonder, as if she has finally surprised herself. "You will remember everything or you will forget. In either event"—she shrugs her shoulders—"it will be exactly the way it should."

She is dead in November. It is the swept clean of autumn in Los Angeles, when the world is a simple equation, blue into blue. The air smells of purity and creation. Perhaps I am relieved. She has been a burden, with her undyed hair falling past her shoulders, with her blue jeans and poncho and sandals, with her unprovable poetry, her vodka and spilled ashtrays and cookies. She is gone and I am free of her cycles of deprivation and excess and that startled look is finally removed from her eyes. I am the only orphan in Westford Academy. I am invited everywhere.

I am prepared to mourn her but find I do not. Instinctively, I know I can trade on her tragedy, can use her death to enlarge my life. I do this with the ease of a child, ruthless, without conscience. I have the conversation piece, the show stopper. It is better than playing the piano or tap dancing. She was hiding a lump the size of an egg in her breast, I say and survive. She bathed with her bra on, it's true, I'm not kidding, I say, and I am always the center of attention. I keep surviving. I am twelve. I am thirteen. My tennis improves, my skiing and French. My mother, who had lived somehow posthumously, at the periphery, always somehow after the fact, is finally and completely gone. I feel I am born for this total eclipse, it feeds me.

I don't know precisely when I was first overtaken by these longings for her. I cannot say when shame and cruelty were transformed into love, what secret bridges must be built or how such structures are devised and crossed. I am much older.

When I am asked the place of my birth, I name the village on the Pacific coast of Mexico where my mother, alone with an infant, wrote poems, lost entirely except for the title. At such moments, sometimes quite unexpectedly, I consider the permutations of squandering the blue. I do not tire of this. I do not think I will ever exhaust these possibilities.

Always, I return to my mother in Maui. What seizure of doubt, of herself and her purpose, must have assaulted her that she would leave the jungle where so little was expected and she was competent, to return to her mother's house in Beverly Hills? Certainly she could foresee how alien this would be, how she would feel suffocated behind the rows of scrubbed greenery, after the unimpeded ocean of Mexico, after the directionless abundance of the Hawaiian jungle, the sunsets with their delicate reds and pagan purples, indelible, like birth. She knew Dominique would be severe and unrelenting. She knew the implication would be that what she did was unsubstantial and useless and her drinking could not but worsen.

I would like to tell her that I understand she did this for me. Mourning was an atrocity. Her sensibility was a curse. She brought me to a place she could not bear and by an act of faith greater than herself, she endured it for years. She gave me back my life before I realized that it was not mine. I did not say thank you. I did not say I love you.

In my mind, she is always traversing a backyard in Beverly Hills, her walk unsolid. In this re-creation, I am not avoiding her eyes, annoyed. I am playing tennis, and this time, I toss my racket away. I say this means nothing. And take the teacups, the ballet and swimming lessons. I do not need them.

In my reinventions, I am not standing in mute banality. I say this life you have given me is of no consequence, not the gray-and-white uniforms, not these houses with their grounds a pathetic suggestion of the tropical. They are outlines without substance. I can do without them.

I am reaching out my hand. I am saying let's go to Cancún or Honolulu, where there are men with long hair and guitars, the kind you once and too briefly loved. Look at how young and strong I am. I can walk for hours, with you, along sea cliffs adorned with permanently wild flowers. You will see that I have a capacity for silence. You will see that I can listen.

I understand that I will never be able to fully comprehend her. I am aware of her vulnerability now. It is not that I romanticize neurosis. It is simply that at last and finally I feel an inexpressible sympathy. I know that whatever is excitable and open in me, all that desires magnitude and grace, this is her legacy.

Of course the things we would most want to say, to change, to soften, the very words that could, in fact, alter the course of our lives or the very orbits of worlds, are the words we cannot say, not then, not later or ever. My mother loved me.

WINTER

BLUES

THERE IS THE SOUND OF RAIN, THERE IS always the sound of rain. It is a Thursday in January in the Northern California town of Cotati in what will be a year of record-breaking cold and floods. It will be the year of Chernobyl. She will always remember the day the nuclear fallout passed over her condominium complex, how thunder was sudden, how a kind of blue ice fell for perhaps fifteen minutes. It was singular, how blue the air became. The news that night didn't mention it.

Erica watched her daughter make snowballs. It was such an astonishment, this cold blue anomaly, that Erica did not think it might be dangerous. One tarnished cell producing a string of pinheads, like a cool tracer bullet through a thousand generations. That did not occur to her then, only later. But now even Chernobyl is months away.

Erica has a paper due in her modern American poetry class. If she can complete this paper on time, she has only one more semester of course work before her teaching credential program. For reasons no one has adequately explained to her, there are vacancies in the fifth grade. She could expect immediate employment.

Erica is trying to type while Flora sits on her lap, while Flora crawls over her and pulls the electric cord from the wall and crumples the pages as she types them. In between, Flora demands pudding. Then she needs macaroni and orange juice. Flora asks for crackers with jam on them. She requires one napkin after another. Erica has learned to make sandwiches and sponge up spilled milk while simultaneously rereading lined-in yellow-crayon passages from a textbook. She has learned to give the appearance of being physically present when in fact she is somewhere else entirely. Or perhaps this is a kind of emotional sleight of hand she always knew. Perhaps it is a rare intrinsic gift, something she was born with.

Now she is attempting to explore the issue of why so many American poets have destroyed themselves and what that tells us about our society. She has chosen Hart Crane, Anne Sexton, and Sylvia Plath as examples. In between she must mix flour and water into a paste for Flora to make collages, for Flora to stick photographs cut from magazines onto sheets of gray construction paper. In between she must change her daughter's clothing, locate sweaters, then a second and third pair of knee socks. She must brush her daughter's hair and teeth.

Erica is thinking about Hart Crane jumping off a ship near Cuba. Suddenly she wants to fall to her knees and pray for the poets. She imagines them with immaculate ravaged faces, with necklaces of ransacked moons, with teeth which are black stubs. Poets are collections of unused crescents and bandages, confused images and terrible departings. They wear poisoned cameos. There is the prophecy of bridges and remote trains.

Flora is pulling the sleeve of her sweater. Flora is asking her to change Barbie doll clothing. Erica struggles to guide the doll arm into the miniature garment. Then Flora asks for ice cream. Erica tells her to get it for herself.

"I can't reach that high," Flora explains. She is patient.

"Get a chair," Erica screams. "Use two hands."

She is always telling Flora to use two hands. It is possible that symmetry is not natural. It is somehow an acquired trait.

"I can't," Flora admits. "I just can't." She looks startled and frightened. She begins to cry.

Erica sighs. It is later, after the ice cream. Erica is drinking Russian vodka straight. She often thinks that the only way she will stop doing this is if someone captures her and somehow sews her mouth shut. Four months later, when she hears that the nuclear reactor at Chernobyl has melted down, her immediate reaction is to drive through Cotati buying bottles of Russian vodka. Just in case the Russian water supply or air becomes so contaminated it affects liquor exports. Just in case they stop making it.

It is eight P.M. The rain has stopped or perhaps, and more likely, merely entered a brief period of remission. And what does the flagrant self-destruction of American poets tell us about the quality of our lives? This is what Erica is thinking as she arranges Flora in front of the television set. She places a white cotton pillow beneath her daughter's head. She surrounds Flora with her favorite stuffed animals, her panda with the velvet paws, her large gray raccoon, and her shaggy white dog with the heart-shaped name tag on a red plastic leash. Flora orders more toys. Erica goes upstairs to collect them. There is the pink bunny that makes music when you shake it, the white-and-black cat with the mouse that sticks to its paws, the drum from Disneyland, crayons and coloring books.

The television is a permanent static at the periphery. It is the new perimeter of her sensibility, a kind of fence or lower register that seems sharp and metallic. She carries her vodka bottle to the window. There is the smear of rain and the abscess of night beyond it. Erica is thinking that poets know there is nothing to see in the sealed sky. The moon is black as a gutter dog. The sky is a kind of zoo. There are no celestial matings.

It is too cold to sleep in their bedrooms upstairs. Flora and Erica have been sleeping together on the living-room floor in front of the fireplace. They lie down with their clothing on in a sleeping bag. Flora falls asleep quickly. Erica listens to the rain. She remembers the city of her birth, Los Angeles, and how she could hear the city breathing. It was some sort of organic ruin, an accident of architecture and brutal necessity. There was an inspired pulse beneath the shell. The iridescence was somehow almost legible, suggesting a calligraphy of exposed bone, transparencies, experimental skin grafts. The blood of Los Angeles was a red neon wash, a kind of sea of autistic traffic lights. In the mockery of stillness, the insistent repetition would clarify itself. It was the sound of transition, not an absence but a seizure of competing postures and rituals. There was abundance where there should be none. It was a form of diversity so distorted and rapid that the sudden mutations were actually audible.

Now there is the density of this other northern night that remembers rivers and forests and rain. Perhaps this night has compassion, this night that is of the elements, the untarnished imperatives of this earth. She considers poets with their heads in ovens, with carbon monoxide hoses in their mouths. It is some final act of alchemy, perhaps, the transmutation of gas and poison into a substance that absolves. There are small blue flames on the kitchen stove. Such blue things anchor worlds. It is always a poet's winter. They stand with their feet at the edge of night bridges. Their toes reach over into the great blue nothing. The world stalls and holds its breath. We are children again. We know the cool blue definitions as a child knows not to cross the road or touch flame. Then we touch it.

It's been weeks without sunlight. Morning is a damp gray, as if there had been a monumental transgression that required an unexpected punishment. She considers the gray of London in 1963. It was raining when Sylvia Plath committed suicide. Perhaps the air was dangerous and wounded. It felt cold and soiled. Plath had shed the world as it actually was. She had penetrated into the inviolate chamber, where the mystery was ceaselessly unraveling across the illusion of cool blue glass. And in the manicured parks, only violets and lilacs and asters. All the colors of bruises, violence and disaster.

Cartoons begin in eight minutes. If she can keep Flora occupied that long, she will be able to sit at her typewriter and consider aspects of self-destruction in the lives of modern American poets, how they have engineered the particles and made the ruinous aesthetic. You could breathe the gas in and it would be a series of individual blue jewels. Suicide would be a kind of clarity, a turquoise definition. It would be like falling in love.

Slabs of granite glow red and explode. The air is torn. Men with deformed faces threaten little girls who wear rings that paralyze and sting. There are hints of incest and perversion. The rules of gravity have been suspended. This is the apocalypse of childhood we carry with us and never forget. Cartoons have begun.

"I'm bored," Flora tells her again. It is later. Flora is pulling on the left side of her sweater.

It was the coldest winter in decades, in England, in 1963. Sylvia Plath had discovered the subtle equation between elements, the slow tidepools and follies of morning. The way there is no north or south. And now there is nothing left for her daughter. They have exhausted the forms of diversion. They haven't left the apartment in more than a week.

"I'm bored here," Flora screams, pulling the typewriter cord from the socket. Her daughter's fists are clenched.

Okay, Erica concedes, leaning against the kitchen wall, pulling on her boots. Okay. We'll go outside. Then she is buttoning Flora's navy blue raincoat and leading her through puddles to the carport. Then she is driving through swollen streets wondering where a woman alone with a child can go in a rainstorm. A woman without a single friend in the county on a January day when a record rainfall will occur.

She is driving north on Petaluma Hill Road. Later, in May, the countryside will be startling with wild yellow flowers advancing to the horizon. Later there will be a soft green wash across the rolling hillsides with their cows, their acres of pasture and sheep. Now the road is a bare suggestion between a gray without seams.

She will take Flora to the Santa Rosa Mall, she decides. The mall is an enclosed area where they can walk and remain dry. The assault of listless color will amuse her daughter. Erica parks in the underground structure and notes that this particular mall is orange brick. It is a kind of morgue for the not yet dead. Flora begins humming.

The mall seems almost deserted. The barrage of oddly

muted neon and garish window displays is somehow halfhearted. They are selling a style of clothing Erica wore before her daughter was born. She allows Flora to run into a toy store. She sits on a bench, smoking a cigarette and listening to rain collide with the roof.

She realizes that she has been wearing the same clothing for days. It's been too cold to change. Her nightgown is a kind of permanent inner layer she tucks into her jeans. And it suddenly occurs to her that she has spent the last four years in one shopping mall or another, on interminable afternoons and weekends, in rain and on holidays. She is always a woman alone with a child in an alien landscape. A woman who does not know a single person in the county.

There was a mall in Maui, in Kahului, near the airport. She would go there after her slow morning walks along the ocean and before the ritual of sunset, when the sky was pagan corals opened and surrendering in a mime of sexual abandon. That was when the sky was the pink of irradiated flamingos and fuchsias. She would drive from the apartment she rented in Lahaina, across the eight-mile strip of ruined sugarcane to the jungle side of the island, to the mall. She could wander unmolested there. When her daughter became tired, she carried Flora in her arms.

Derek wasn't living with them. He was staying in a shack without electricity in the jungle. He was becoming a pot farmer near Hana. He came to see them in Lahaina at Christmas. He was lying on the sofa watching football on television. Then he was screaming that he couldn't stand it.

She carried her vodka glass into the hallway. The glass had become almost part of her body, like another appendage. It seemed organic and effortless. Derek was in the bathroom, his eyes narrow with rage. "I can't use a flush toilet," he said. "I've lived outside so long I get cramps if I don't squat." He was staring at her as if this was somehow her fault. She was always compromising him. She blanched at international borders. She trembled when customs agents opened her suitcases. Now there was the matter of the child. Derek kicked the door and the wood split.

Then it was late afternoon in the Kahului Mall. Flora spent hours staring at parrots and hamsters. Her daughter's capacity for the pet shop was limitless. Their afternoons were informed by canaries and puppies, turtles and gold-fish. Flora remained indifferent to landscapes, to the in-toxicated air, the way the skies seemed lava, primal and unsubtle. Flora was perfunctory in response to waterfalls, macadamia groves, cliffs of ti plants, and stalks of torch ginger. Flora did not care if they lived inside a postcard. Flora was watching a kitten sleep.

The Kahului Mall was a kind of DMZ. Here she was simply a nameless shopper without history or resonance. She was an anonymous woman with a child who had some-how come to the islands and would go. She was merely a woman holding a net shopping bag, glancing at the price tags on aloha print dresses. She was camouflaged and in-violate. She smoked on the bench outside the pet shop. The pet shop smelled of grit and mystery and childhood. The fish tanks were dark and cool and seemed vast, the way a movie theater did on a Saturday when she was seven. Now Erica carried a soda bottle filled with vodka. She ac-cepted a card for a free lei-making class, for a series of hula lessons. Derek was in the jungle and he wasn't coming back.

Erica walks into the toy store in the Santa Rosa Mall. It is two years later. Flora wants more Barbie doll dresses, evening gowns, bridal ensembles, and cocktail party skirts. She has selected a Barbie office outfit with a tailored jacket and knee-high red boots. She also wants an expensive mock medical kit with a clever toy stethoscope inside, a plastic thermometer, realistic eye chart, and rubber syringe. Erica agrees to buy it.

They are home in the early afternoon. There is no way to fill up this day. She turns on cartoons for her daughter. She thinks of the wine country she has just driven through, how the weight of it feels like a violation. She has never been graceful with transitions.

Her husband, Derek, had an ease with borders. With him she knew it was all simply a matter of color and angles, of love affairs begun and ended at airports. They had portable identities. She carried several passports in her purse, mosquito repellent, cash, a Swiss army knife, and a paper fan. There was no terrain that could surprise.

Erica considers Derek and the hotel rooms that lie between them. Always a shuttered window is opening onto an alley or a plaza with a monument, bronze soldiers school children leave tulips for. There are mountains beyond the city. It is India or France or Peru. Derek has removed the cameras from his neck, the many eyes he thinks justify him. He has fallen across a sofa as if harpooned. He will remain that way indefinitely. In between she will make herself smell expensive. She will put on lipstick, kohl, and high heels. She will put on pearls and a silk scarf at her neck. She will visit doctors and collect codeine prescriptions for him.

Derek will not tour the museum or take her to dinner. Beyond the hotel window, up a hill, are the ruins of a city Homer mentioned. Derek is watching "Hawaii Five-0" on television. It is dubbed in a language he does not speak. He studies the edges of frames, searching for something familiar. He is transfixed, as if he expected to encounter old friends.

She is watching him. She is always at the edge, too, watching him. She is drinking vodka and pain pills. Derek would be gone for months in the desert or mountains or

jungle. Then he would send for her. He would watch television relentlessly. There would be constant room service.
This was his concept of the civilization he rejected. Always,
he was turning their hotel rooms into convalescent homes.
He is immobile on clean sheets, trays collect. When he is
stronger, he will order newspapers and magazines. He is
lying in one bed or another like an invalid.

She can remember the smell of his flesh. It seemed
coated with a fine dust, some residue from alleys in villages
eight thousand years old. And market stalls and bells from
churches, a sense of music escaping from the mosques.
There are sails on one blue horizon or another and piers
with the sound of wind in tin. Always there are the fishing
nets pulled in after dusk. And she thinks of Maui, with the
ocean blue beyond blue, livid, newly formed. It was on the
other side of the lanai. It needed neither purpose nor jus-
tification. It was a blue beyond the postcards. The sea and
jungle resisted reproduction. The actual colors were an ex-
travagance beyond the camera. Hawaii could not make itself small and conventional enough for the lens. Nothing
could accommodate the glare of the plumeria. Or the green
in all its permutations, uninhibited, rebellious, startling.
And the ocean, with its ruthless and implacable incaution.
After a time, Derek stopped taking photographs.

Flora asks her to switch television stations. Then she
wants her to change Barbie doll dresses. She insists that
Erica find missing doll garments, that she coordinate
dresses with the appropriate shoes.

Erica considers throwing Barbie against the wall, or yank-
ing out her arms, or biting through the neck. She could
sever the head of that icon of anorexia. Instead, Erica opens
the new medical kit, the one Flora begged her for and now
doesn't want to play with. Erica touches the stethoscope
and then the rubber syringe.

"Barbie needs a fix," Erica says. "Help her out."

"Is that a joke?" Flora stares at her. She places her hands on her hips.

"Yes." Erica is drinking vodka and smoking a cigarette. It is still afternoon. It is still raining.

"It's not funny," Flora decides. She turns her back on her mother and slowly walks away.

Erica sits at her typewriter, considering Sylvia Plath in London in winter. And Anne Sexton in Boston. They also had daughters. They must have worn their nightgowns all day. Or perhaps they wore their other lives like cotton frocks in a pastel simultaneity. Then they forgot the calla lilies, the Sunday church bells, the afternoons of white moths and lies that clarified and defined them like a perfect translation.

Later Flora wants to be a princess. Erica must adjust veils and devise a method of attaching lace curtains to her daughter's shoulder. She must create a train that is dramatic and functional. It is still raining. It is after dinner. Erica carries the vodka bottle with her from room to room.

They have been sleeping in front of the fireplace for warmth. Now they are out of wood. Erica carries her daughter upstairs to her bedroom. She puts a fresh red sweater on her daughter. She brushes Flora's teeth and hair. She places her daughter in bed. Then she closes the closet door against the possibility of demons and ghosts. She reaches down and turns on the night-light, an ornate bulb surrounded by cowrie shells. Derek bought it for Flora one August afternoon in Lahania. Now Erica has given Flora the seven magic kisses for under her pillow. She imparts the seven magic kisses on each cheek.

"You forgot my brain kiss," Flora informs her.

Erica was standing near the door. She returns, sits on

her daughter's bed, kisses her forehead. I'm not going to get through this, she thinks.

"What about my foot kisses?" Flora is staring at her.

Erica extracts her daughter's legs one at a time. She kisses the soles of her feet. Erica has already placed a glass of apple juice on the table beside her bed. She has already rubbed her daughter's back until the dark brown eyes began to close. Flora has already said her prayers.

"I want a bedtime story," Flora reveals. "Tell me about you and Daddy and the rats."

Erica takes a breath. "The rats in Nepal? In Katmandu?" she asks. "We used to feed them twice a day, like cats. We just put food out on a plate for them. We had rats in India, too. There was typhoid. We were a twelve-day hike from the doctor. Not a real doctor. A missionary who might have some training."

"Tell me about the mosquito nets." Flora is smiling.

"Daddy didn't believe in them, not even in East Africa. He said anything that bit him would die from the toxins," Erica says.

"I want to hear about the gun," Flora says, her voice soft.

"You remember that story?"

Flora laughs. "Yes."

"It was a fishing village in the south of Spain. We rented a car. I was driving," Erica says, squinting, as if she can see it better that way. "Daddy was too sick to drive. We heard there were Peace Corps people in the mountains. That was the rumor. We got there and they knew next to nothing about the poppy trade."

"They were vegetarians," Flora tells her.

"Yes. You remember everything. And they had no idea which doctors in Valenica would write prescriptions or which pharmacies would fill them."

"Then what?" Flora closes her eyes.

"Daddy took out a pistol and pointed it at them. 'If I find there's smack around you haven't told me about, I'll come back and kill you,' he said. Then he pointed the gun at me and said, 'Is it true?' I said, 'Believe him.'"

"Daddy really wanted that smack," Flora says.

"Yes." It is still raining.

"What's smack?" Flora asks.

Erica considers the possibilities. "It's a kind of poison," she says.

Is it possible that it is raining even harder? It is a permanent damp night. In Spain, twenty years ago, Derek was too sick to drive. Later that evening, she put on a silk suit and pearls. She told the doctor at the emergency hospital that she was a tourist with a bad back. She had left her pills in Paris. Then she was smiling, gracefully opening a leather wallet and removing cash.

"Is Daddy coming back?" Flora asks.

The wind is howling. They are out of firewood. And she is a long way from the tropics, from the particular corrupt heat that nourished her. There is nothing on the other side of the window but the cold dull night and the moon who moans in all dialects and forgets nothing.

If it continues to storm, she won't even be able to drive Flora to the Santa Rosa Mall. She has heard on the radio that Highway 101 is closed in both directions, that the alternative roads have washed away. Bridges across the Russian River are gone. People are stranded in the hills. She remembers how she looked today, reflected in a shop mirror, how long and gray her hair is, how strange she looks, with a nightgown stuffed into her jeans, with a flannel shirt and wool sweater and down jacket on.

She remembers Derek in her apartment in Lahaina. It is the day before she left Maui. Derek is banging on the door.

He is ringing the bell and yelling. It is not yet dawn. He is kicking the door. He has a knife in his hand.

"Cut me," he says when she opens the door. He indicates a spot on his leg.

Erica stares at his leg. She looks at the knife. "I beg your pardon?"

"Cut me." Derek is insistent. He points at his leg. "You can do it. Cut me enough so I go to the hospital. If I need stitches, they'll give me codeine."

Flora has woken up. Erica holds their daughter. She looks into her husband's eyes. It is a door into a corridor she no longer wishes to enter.

"Cut yourself," she decided. "Cut your throat."

"Is Daddy coming back?" Flora repeats.

She says, "No."

Erica stands in the living room. Then she sits by the fireplace which is filled with yesterday's ashes. Erica cannot imagine any mechanism by which this winter will ever end, this rain and this night and its exquisitely venomous sisters.

It is winter in Los Angeles, in the city of her birth. The moon there is full, tranquil, and undamaged. In Los Angeles she had a house on a hillside. There were pale butterflies in the backyard above bougainvillea and freshly risen stalks of bamboo. The night was vivid with a fascination of purple jasmine, kisses and lamps and the ambiguous scent of amber. The abstract avenues were informed by the small coherence of jacaranda rising like twin columns on both sides of the street, erasing the concept of leaving or arriving.

It is four or five months from Chernobyl and the blue rain that will deposit its strange ice in her yard, the day the fallout the authorities called harmless passed above Sonoma county. The day the sky ached. The next morning she will drive through Cotati buying Russian vodka, just in case.

It is less than a year from the October when she will, quite by accident, attend a meeting of Alcoholics Anonymous and get sober.

Now there is a kind of snap and the lights go out. The electricity will remain down for six days. She is out of firewood. She sits alone in the dark.

Erica thinks about the lives of American poets in this century. They leap from bridges and ships. It is an elongated January of derelict inventions, of perpetual mourning and amulets. The poets put their heads in ovens. They are drawn to the pulse of the blue flame. Their skulls are plazas of grief and rotting. They have depots and piers inside their eyes. There is the terrible heartbreak of going. Then they put the carbon monoxide in their mouths. Always they are sick beneath a devious scripture of moon. It is a season of crimes. They are wearing their diseases like garlands, necklaces of plumeria. They walk in circles in shopping malls. They are searching for something ineluctable and they are never certain. Then they leave their children orphans.

The only light in the house is the match that lights her cigarette. And it occurs to her that the only light in the world is the flame that is killing us.

TALL TALES

FROM THE

MEKONG DELTA

I T WAS IN THE FIFTH MONTH OF HER SOBRI-
ety. It was after the hospital. It was after her divorce. It
was autumn. She had even stopped smoking. She was wearing pink aerobic pants, a pink T-shirt with KAUAI written in
lilac across the chest, and tennis shoes. She had just come
from the gym. Her black hair was damp. She was wearing
a pink sweatband around her forehead. She was walking
across a parking lot bordering a city park in West Hollywood. She was carrying cookies for the AA meeting. She
was in charge of bringing the food for the meeting. He fell
into step with her. He was short, fat, pale. He had bad teeth.
His hair was dirty. Later, she would freeze this frame in
her mind and study it. She would say he seemed frightened
and defeated and trapped, cagey was the word she used to
describe his eyes, how he measured and evaluated something in the air between them. The way he squinted
through hazel eyes, it had nothing to do with the sunlight.

"I'm Lenny," he said, extending his hand. "What's your name?"

She told him. She was holding a bag with packages of cookies in it. After the meeting, she had an appointment with her psychiatrist, then a manicure. She kept walking.

"You a teacher? You look like a teacher," he said.

"I'm a writer," she told him. "I teach creative writing."

"You look like a teacher," Lenny said.

"I'm not just a teacher," she told him. She was annoyed.

"Okay. You're a writer. And you're bad. You're one of those bad girls from Beverly Hills. I've had my eye on you," Lenny said.

She didn't say anything. He was wearing blue jeans, a black leather jacket zipped to his throat, a long red wool scarf around his neck, and a Dodgers baseball cap. It was too hot a day for the leather jacket and scarf. She didn't find that detail significant. It caught her attention, she touched it briefly and then let it go. She looked but did not see. They were standing on a curb. The meeting was in a community room across the boulevard. She wasn't afraid yet.

"You do drugs? What do you do? Drink too much?" he asked.

"I'm a cocaine addict," she told him.

"Me too. Let's see your tracks. Show me your tracks." Lenny reached out for her arm.

"I don't have any now." She glanced at her arm. She extended her arm into the yellow air between them. The air was already becoming charged and disturbed. "They're gone."

"I see them," Lenny told her, inspecting her arm, turning it over, holding it in the sunlight. He touched the part of her arm behind her elbow where the vein rose. "They're beautiful."

"But there's nothing there," she said.

"Yeah, there is. There always is if you know how to look,"
Lenny told her. "How many people by the door? How many
steps?"

He was talking about the door across the boulevard. His
back was turned. She didn't know.

"Four steps," Lenny said. "Nine people. Four women.
One old man. I look. I see."

She was counting the people on the steps in front of the
meeting. She didn't say anything.

"Let's get coffee later. That's what you do, right? You
can't get a drink? You go out for coffee?" Lenny was studying her face.

"I don't think so," she said.

"You don't think so? Come on. I'll buy you coffee. You
can explain AA to me. You like that Italian shit? That
French shit? The little cups?" Lenny was staring at her.

"No, thank you. I'm sorry," she said. He was short and
fat and sweating. He looked like he was laughing at her with
his eyes.

"You're sorry. I'll show you sorry. Listen. I know what
you want. You're one of those smart ass teachers from Beverly Hills," Lenny said.

"Right," she said. She didn't know why she bothered talking to him.

"You want to get in over your head. You want to see
what's on the other side. I'll show you. I'll take you there.
It'll be the ride of your life," Lenny said.

"Good-bye," she answered.

Lenny was at her noon meeting the next day.
She saw him as she walked through the door. She wondered

how he knew that she would be there. As she approached
her usual chair, she saw a bouquet of long-stemmed pink
roses.

"You look beautiful," Lenny said. "You knew I'd be here.
That's why you put that crap on your face. You didn't have
that paint on yesterday. Don't do that. You don't need that.
Those whores from Beverly Hills need it. Not you. You're
a teacher. I like that. Sit down." He picked the roses up.
"Sit next to me. You glad to see me?"

"I don't think so." She sat down. Lenny handed the roses
to her. She put them on the floor.

"Yeah. You're glad to see me. You were hoping I'd be
here. And here I am. You want me to chase you? I'll chase
you. Then I'll catch you. Then I'll show you what being in
over your head means." Lenny was smiling.

She turned away. When the meeting was over, she stood
up quickly and began moving, even before the prayer was
finished. "I have to go," she said, softly, over her shoulder.
She felt she had to apologize. She felt she had to be careful.

"You don't have to go," Lenny said. He caught up with
her on the steps. "Yeah. Don't look surprised. Lenny's fast,
real fast. And you're lying. Don't ever lie to me. You think
I'm stupid? Yeah, you think Lenny's stupid. You think you
can get away from me? You can't get away. You got an
hour. You don't pick that kid up for the dance school until
four. Come on. I'll buy you coffee."

"What are you talking about?" She stopped. Her breath
felt sharp and fierce. It was a warm November. The air felt
like glass.

"That kid. That your daughter? You take her to dance
school every Wednesday at four," Lenny said.

"How do you know that?" She put her hands on her hips.

"I know all about you. I know your routine. I been watching you for two weeks. Ever since I got to town. I saw you

my first day. You think I'd ask you out on a date and not know your routine?" Lenny stared at her.

She felt her eyes widen. She started to say something but she changed her mind.

"You live at the top of the hill, off of Doheny. You pick up that kid, what's her name, Annie something? You pick her up and take her to dance school. You get coffee next door. Table by the window. You read the paper. Then you go home. Just the two of you. And that Mex cleaning lady. Maria. That her name? Maria? They're all called Maria. And the gardener Friday afternoons. That's it." Lenny lit a cigarette.

"You've been following me?" She was stunned. Her mouth opened.

"Recon," Lenny said.

"I beg your pardon?"

"In Nam. We called it recon. Fly over, get a lay of the land. Or stand behind some trees. Count the personnel. People look but they don't see. I'll tell you about it. Get coffee. You got an hour. Want to hear about Vietnam? I got stories. Choppers? I like choppers. You can take your time, aim. You can hit anything, even dogs. Some days we'd go out just aiming at dogs. Or the black market? Want to hear about that? Profiteering in smack? You're a writer, right? You like stories. I got some tall tales from the Mekong Delta for you, sweetheart. Knock your socks off. Come on." He reached out and touched her arm. "Later you can have your own war stories. I can be one of your tall tales. I can be the tallest."

The sun was strong. The world was washed with white. The day seemed somehow clarified. He was wearing a leather jacket and shaking. It occurred to her that he was sick.

"Excuse me. I must go," she said. "If you follow me, I shall have someone call the police."

"Okay. Okay. Calm down," Lenny was saying behind her. "I'll save you a seat tomorrow, okay?"

She didn't reply. She sat in her car. It was strange how blue the sky seemed, etched with the blue of radium or narcotics. Or China blue, perhaps. Was that a color? The blue of the China Sea? The blue of Vietnam. When he talked about Asia, she could imagine that blue, luminescent with ancient fever, with bridges broken, with the harvest lost in blue flame.

She locked her car and began driving. It occurred to her, suddenly, that the Chinese took poets as concubines. Their poets slept with warlords. They wrote with gold ink. They ate orchids and smoked opium. They were consecrated by nuance, by birds and silk and the ritual birthdays of gods and nothing changed for a thousand years. And afternoon was absinthe yellow and almond, burnt orange and chrysanthemum. And in the abstract sky, a litany of kites.

She felt herself look for him as she walked into the meeting the next day at noon. The meeting was in the basement of a church. The room was dark and cool. There were long tables in the center of the room. Lenny was standing near the coffeepot with his back to the wall. He was holding two cups of coffee as if he was expecting her. He handed one to her.

"I got seats," he said. He motioned for her to follow. She followed. He pointed to a chair. She sat in it. An older woman was standing at the podium, telling the story of her life. Lenny was wearing a white warm-up suit with a green neon stripe down the sides of the pants and the arms of the jacket. He was wearing a baseball cap. His face seemed younger and tanner than she had remembered.

"Like how I look? I look like a lawyer on his way to tennis, right? I even got a tan. Fit right in. Chameleon Lenny. The best, too." He lit a cigarette. He held the pack out to her.

She shook her head, no. She was staring at the cigarette in his mouth, in his fingers. She could lean her head closer, part her lips, take just one puff.

"I got something to show you," Lenny said.

The meeting was over. The older woman had finished telling her story. At the long tables, they were clapping. The older woman had blond hair pulled into a tight bun and large pearl earrings. She was wearing a suit and blue shoes. She did not look like she had ever had a problem with drugs or alcohol or anything else.

They were walking up the stairs from the basement of the church. The sun was strong. She blinked in the light. It was the yellow of a hot autumn, a yellow that seemed amplified and redeemed. She glanced at her watch.

"Don't do that," Lenny said. He was touching the small of her back with his hand. He was helping her walk.

"What?"

"Look at that fucking watch all the time. Take if off," Lenny said.

"My watch?" She was looking at her wrist as if she had never seen it before.

"Give it here, come on." Lenny put his hand out. He motioned with his fingers. She placed her watch in the palm of his hand.

"That's a good girl," Lenny was saying. "You don't need it. You don't have to know what time it is. You're with me. Don't you get it? You're hungry, I feed you. You're tired, I find a hotel. You're in a structured environment now.

You're protected. I protect you. It doesn't matter what time it is." He put her watch in his pocket. "Forget it. I'll buy you a new one. A better one. That was junk. I was embarrassed for you to wear junk like that. Want a Rolex?"

"You can't afford a Rolex," she said. She felt intelligent. She looked into his face.

"I got a drawerful," Lenny told her. "I got all the colors. Red. Black. Gold."

"Where?" She studied his face. They were walking on a side street in Hollywood. The air was a pale blue, bleeding into the horizon, taking the sky.

"In the bank," Lenny said. "In the safety deposit with everything else. All the cash that isn't buried." Lenny smiled.

"What else?" She put her hands on her hips.

"Let's go for a ride," Lenny said.

They were standing at the curb. They were two blocks from the church. A motorcycle was parked there. Lenny took out a key.

"Get on," he said.

"I don't want to get on a motorcycle." She was afraid.

"Yes, you do." Lenny told her.

"No, I don't."

"Sit down on it. Wrap your arms around me. Just lean into me. Nothing else. You'll like it. You'll be surprised. It's a beautiful day. It looks like Hong Kong today. Want to go to the beach? Want lunch? I know a place in Malibu. You like seafood? Crab? Scampi? Watch the waves?" Lenny was doing something to the motorcycle. He looked at her face.

"No," she said.

"How about Italian? I got a place near the Marina. Owner owes for ten kilos. We'll get a good table. You like linguini?" Lenny sat down on the motorcycle.

She shook her head, no.

"Okay. You're not hungry. You're skinny. You should eat. Come on. We'll go around the block. Get on. Once around the block and I'll bring you back to the church." Lenny reached out his hand through the warm white air.

She looked at his hand and how the air seemed blue near his fingers. It's simply a blue glaze, she was thinking. And the sides are a kind of blue gauze, taping the wound of the world. In Malibu, in Hilo, in the China Sea, forms of blue, confusion and remorse, a dancing dress, a daughter with a mouth precisely your own and it's done, all of it.

Somewhere it was carnival night in the blue wash of a village on the China Sea. On the river, boats passed with low slung antique masts sliding silently to the blue of the ocean, to the inverted delta where the horizon concluded itself in a rapture of orchid and pewter. That's what she was thinking when she took his hand.

She did not see him for a week. She changed her meeting schedule. She went to women's meetings in the Pacific Palisades and the Valley. She went to meetings she had never been to before. She trembled when she thought about him.

She stopped her car at a red light. It occurred to her that it was an early afternoon in late autumn in her thirty-eighth year and she could explain everything. Someone stands on a balcony counting red camellias in terra-cotta pots. Someone smiles at the camera. Someone else jumps. That is all.

Then she found herself driving to the community center. The meeting was over. There was no one left on the street. Just one man, sitting alone on the front steps, smoking. He looked up at her and smiled.

"I was expecting you," Lenny said. "I told you. You can't get away from me."

She could feel his eyes on her face, the way she had learned to feel lamplight on her skin when she lived with a painter. When she had learned to perceive light as an entity. She began to cry.

"Don't cry," Lenny said, his voice soft. "I can't stand you crying. Let's make up. I'll buy you dinner."

"I can't." She didn't look at him.

"Yeah. You can. I'll take you someplace good. Spago? You like those little pizzas with the duck and shit? Lobster? You want the Palm? The Rangoon Racket Club? Yeah. Don't look so surprised. I know the places. I made deals in all those places. What did you think?" She could feel his eyes on her skin.

She didn't say anything. They were walking across a parking lot. She looked at the houses beyond the fence and it seemed to her that the landscape was somehow redundant and impermanent. The late autumn made everything ache. Later, it would be worse. At dusk, with the subtle irritation of lamps.

"Yeah. I know what you think. You think Lenny looks like he just crawled out from a rock. This is a disguise. Blue jeans, sneakers. I fit right in. I got a gang of angry Colombians on my ass. Forget it." Lenny stared at her. "You got a boyfriend?"

"What's it to you?"

"What's it to me? That's sharp. I want to date you. I probably want to marry you. You got a boyfriend, I got to hurt him." Lenny smiled.

"I can't believe you said that." She put her hands on her hips.

"You got a boyfriend? I'm going to cut off his arm and beat him with it. Here. Look at this." He was bending over and removing something from his sock. He held it in the palm of his hand.

"Know what this is?" Lenny asked.

She shook her head, no.

"It's a knife, sweetheart," Lenny said.

She could see that now, even before he opened it. A push-button knife. Lenny was reaching behind to his back. He was pulling out something from behind his belt, under his shirt. It was another knife.

"Want to see the guns?"

She felt dizzy. They were standing near her car. She leaned against the door. It was hot. It was early in December. The Santa Anas had been blowing. She felt that it had been exceptionally warm for months.

"Don't get in the car," Lenny said. "I can't take it when you leave. Stay near me. Just let me breathe the same air as you. I love you."

"You don't even know me," she said.

"But you know me. You been dreaming me. I'm your ticket to the other side, remember?" Lenny had put his knives away. "Want to hear some more Nam stories? How we ran smack into Honolulu? You'll like this. You like the dope stories. You want to get loaded?"

She shook her head, no.

"You kidding me? You don't want to get high?" Lenny smiled.

"I like being sober," she said.

"Sure," Lenny said. "Let me know when that changes. One phone call. I got the best dope in the world."

They were standing in front of her car. The street beyond the parking lot seemed estranged, the air tarnished. She wondered where the syllables of tenderness were. She hadn't thought about drugs in months. Lenny was handing her something, thin circles of metal. She looked down at her hand. Two dimes seemed to glare in her palm.

"For when you change your mind," Lenny said. He was still smiling.

They were sitting on the grass of a public park after a meeting. Lenny was wearing Bermuda shorts and a green T-shirt that said CANCÚN. They were sitting in a corner of the park with a stucco wall behind them.

"It's our anniversary," Lenny told her. "We been in love four weeks."

"I've lost track of time," she said. She didn't have a watch anymore. The air felt humid, green, stalled. It was December in West Hollywood. She was thinking that the palms were livid with green death. They could be the palms of Vietnam.

"I want to fuck you," Lenny said. "Let's go to your house."

She shook her head, no. She turned away from him. She began to stand up.

"Okay. Okay. You got the kid. I understand that. Let's go to a hotel. You want the Beverly Wilshire? I got a problem there. What about the Four Seasons? You want to fuck in the Four Seasons?"

"You need to get an AIDS test," she said.

"Why?" Lenny looked amused.

"Because you're a heroin addict. Because you've been in jail," she began.

"Who told you that?" Lenny sat up.

"You told me," she said. "Terminal Island. Chino. Folsom? Is it true?"

"Uh-huh," Lenny said. He lit a cigarette. "Five years in Folsom. Consecutive. Sixty months. I topped out."

She stared at him. She thought how easy it would be, to reach out and take a cigarette. Just one, once.

"Means I finished my whole sentence. No time off for good behavior. Lenny did the whole sixty." He smiled. "I don't need an AIDS test."

"You're a heroin addict. You shoot cocaine. You're crazy. Who knows what you do or who you do it with?" She was beginning to be afraid.

"You think I'd give you a disease?" Lenny looked hurt.

Silence. She was looking at Lenny's legs, how white the exposed skin was. She was thinking that he brought his sick body to her, that he was bloated, enormous with pathology and bad history, with jails and demented resentments.

"Listen. You got nothing to worry about. I don't need a fucking AIDS test. Listen to me. Are you hearing me? You get that disease, I take care of you. I take you to Bangkok. I keep a place there, on the river. Best smack in the world. Fifty cents. I keep you loaded. You'll never suffer. You start hurting, I'll take you out. I'll kill you myself. With my own hands. I promise," Lenny said.

Silence. She was thinking that he must be drawn to her vast emptiness, could he sense that she was aching and hot and always listening? Always there is a garish carnival across the boulevard. We are born, we eat and sleep, conspire and mourn, a birth, a betrayal, an excursion to the harbor, and it's done. All of it, done.

"Come here." Lenny extended his arm. "Come here. You're like a child. Don't be afraid. I want to give you something."

She moved her body closer to his. There are blue enormities, she was thinking, horizons and boulevards. Somewhere, there are blue rocks and they burn.

"Close your eyes," Lenny said. "Open your mouth."

She closed her eyes. She opened her mouth. There was something pressing against her lip. Perhaps it was a flower.

"Close your mouth and breathe," Lenny said.

It was a cigarette. She felt the smoke in her lungs. It had been six months since she smoked. Her hand began to tremble.

"There," Lenny was saying. "You need to smoke. I can tell. It's okay. You can't give up everything at once. Here. Share it. Give me a hit."

They smoked quietly. They passed the cigarette back and forth. She was thinking that she was like a sacked capital. Nothing worked in her plazas. The palm trees were on fire. The air was smoky and blue. No one seemed to notice.

"Sit on my lap. Come on. Sit down. Closer. On my lap," Lenny was saying. "Good. Yeah. Good. I'm not going to bite you. I love you. Want to get married? Want to have a baby? Closer. Let me kiss you. You don't do anything. Let me do it. Now your arms. Yeah. Around my neck. Tighter. Tighter. You worried? You got nothing to worry about. You get sick, I keep you whacked on smack. Then I kill you. So what are you worried? Closer. Yeah. Want to hear about R&R in Bangkok? Want to hear about what you get for a hundred bucks on the river? You'll like this. Lean right up against me. Yeah. Close your eyes."

"Look. It's hot. You want to swim? You like that? Swimming? You know how to swim?" Lenny looked at her. "Yeah? Let's go. I got a place in Bel Air."

"You have a place in Bel Air?" she asked. It was after the meeting. It was the week before Christmas. It was early afternoon.

"Guy I used to know, I did a little work for him. I introduced him to his wife. He owes me some money. He gave me the keys." Lenny reached in his pocket. He was wearing a white-and-yellow warm-up suit. He produced a key ring. It hung in the hot air between them. "It's got everything there. Food. Booze. Dope. Pool. Tennis court. Computer games. You like that? Pac Man?"

She didn't say anything. She felt she couldn't move. She lit a cigarette. She was buying two packages at a time again. She would be buying cartons soon.

"Look. We'll go for a drive. I'll tell you some more war stories. How we set that captain from Ohio up? And took him down? He was in a thousand bits but dying slow. And lucid. He put the whole thing together. You could see it in his eyes. You like that story, right? Come on. I got a nice car today. I got a brand-new red Ferrari. Want to see it? Just take a look. One look. It's at the curb. Give me your hand." Lenny reached out for her hand.

She could remember being a child. It was a child's game in a child's afternoon, before time or distance were factors. When you were told you couldn't move or couldn't see. And for those moments you are paralyzed or blind. You freeze in place. You don't move. You feel that you have been there for years. It does not occur to you that you can move. It does not occur to you that you can break the rules. The world is a collection of absolutes and spells. You know words have a power. You are entranced. The world is a soft blue.

"There. See. I'm not crazy. A red Ferrari. A hundred forty grand. Get in. We'll go around the block. Sit down. Nice interior, huh? Nice stereo. But I got no fucking tapes. Go to the record store with me? You pick out the tapes, okay? Then we'll go to Bel Air. Swim a little. Watch the sunset. Listen to some music. Want to dance? I love to dance. You can't get a disease doing that, right?" Lenny was holding the car door open for her.

She sat down. The ground seemed enormous. It seemed to leap up at her face.

"Yeah. I'm a good driver. Lean back. Relax. I used to drive for a living," Lenny told her.

"What did you drive? A bus?" She smiled.

"A bus? That's sharp. You're sharp. You're one of those sharp little Jewish girls from Beverly Hills with a cocaine problem. Yeah. I know what you're about. All of you. I drove some cars on a few jobs. Couple of jewelry stores, a few banks. Now I fly," Lenny said.

Lenny turned the car onto Sunset Boulevard. In the gardens of the houses behind the gates, everything was in bloom. Patches of color slid past so fast she thought they might be hallucinations. Azaleas and camellias and hibiscus. The green seemed sullen and half-asleep. Or perhaps it was opiated, dazed, exhausted from pleasure.

"You fly?" she repeated.

"Planes. You like planes? I'll take you up. I got a plane. Company plane," Lenny told her. "It's in Arizona."

"You're a pilot?" She put out her cigarette and immediately lit another.

"I fly planes for money. Want to fly? I'm going next week. Every second Tuesday. Want to come?" Lenny looked at her.

"Maybe," she said. They had turned on a street north of Sunset. They were winding up a hill. The street was narrow. The bougainvillea was a kind of net near her face. The air smelled of petals and heat.

"Yeah. You'll come with me. I'll show you what I do. I fly over a stretch of desert looks like the moon. There's a small manufacturing business down there. Camouflaged. You'd never see it. I drop some boxes off. I pick some boxes up. Three hours' work. Fifteen grand," Lenny said. "Know what I'm talking about?"

"No."

"Yeah. You don't want to know anything about this. Distribution," Lenny said. "That's federal."

"You do that twice a month?" she asked. They were above Sunset Boulevard. The bougainvillea was a magenta web. There were the sounds of birds and insects. They were winding through pine trees. "That's thirty thousand dollars a month."

"That's nothing. The real money's the Bogotá run," Lenny said. "Mountains leap up out of the ground, out of nowhere. The Bogotá run drove me crazy. Took me a month to come down. Then the Colombians got mad. You know what I'm talking about?"

"No."

"That's good. You don't want to know anything about the Colombians," Lenny said.

She was thinking about the Colombians and Bogotá and the town where Lenny said he had a house, Medellín. She was thinking they would have called her *gitana*, with her long black hair and bare feet. She could have fanned herself with handfuls of hundred-dollar bills like a green river. She could have borne sons for men crossing borders, searching for the definitive run, the one you don't return from. She would dance in bars in the permanently hot nights. They would say she was intoxicated with grief and dead husbands. Sadness made her dance. When she thought about this, she laughed.

The driveway seemed sudden and steep. They were approaching a walled villa. An iron gate went across the driveway. The black bars were pointed at the top, like a series of spears tipped with gold. Lenny pushed numbers on a console. The gate opened.

He parked the red Ferrari. She followed him up a flight of stone steps. The house looked like a Spanish fortress. There were balconies outside the high windows. There were turrets. There was the sound of birds.

A large Christmas wreath with pine cones and a red ribbon hung on the door. The door was unlocked. They walked in. The living room was vast and cool. The floor was tile. They were walking on an Oriental silk carpet, past a piano, a fireplace, a bar. There were ceiling-high glass cabinets in which Chinese artifacts were displayed, vases and bowls and carvings. They were walking through a library, then a room with a huge television, stereo equipment, a pool table. She followed him out a side door.

The pool was built on the edge of the hill. The city below seemed like a sketch for a village, something not quite formed beneath the greenery. Pink and yellow roses had been planted around two sides of the pool. There were beds of azaleas with ferns between them and red camellias, yellow lilies, white daisies, and bird of paradise.

"Time to swim," Lenny said.

She was standing near the pool, motionless. "We don't have suits," she said.

"Don't tell nobody, okay?" Lenny was pulling his shirt over his head. He stared at her, a cigarette in his mouth. "It's private. It's walled. Just a cliff out here. And Bernie and Phyllis aren't coming back. Come on. Take off your clothes. What are you? Scared? You're like a child. Come here. I'll help you. Daddy'll help you. Just stand near me. Here. See? Over your head. Over baby's head. Did that hurt? What's that? One of those goddamn French jobs with the hooks in front? You do it. What are you looking at? I put on a few pounds. Okay? I'm a little out of shape. I need some weights. I got to buy some weights. What are you? Skinny? You're so skinny. You one of those vomiters? I'm not going to bite. Come here. Reach down. Take off my necklace. Unlock the chain. Yeah. Good. Now we swim."

The water felt strange and icy. It was nothing like she expected. There were shadows on the far side of the pool. The shadows were hideous. There was nothing ambiguous about them. The water beneath the shadows looked remote and troubled and green. It looked contaminated. The more she swam, the more the infected blue particles clustered on her skin. There would be no way to remove them.

"I have to leave," she said.

The sun was going down. It was an unusual sunset for Los Angeles, red and protracted. Clouds formed islands in the red sky. The sprinklers came on. The air smelled damp and green like a forest. There were pine trees beyond the rose garden. She thought of the smell of camp at nightfall, when she was a child.

"What are you? Crazy? You kidding me? I want to take you out," Lenny said. He got out of the pool. He wrapped a towel around his waist. Then he wrapped a towel around her shoulders. "Don't just stand there. Dry off. Come on. You'll get sick. Dry yourself."

He lit a cigarette for her. "You want to get dressed up, right? I know you skinny broads from Beverly Hills. You want to get dressed up. Look. Let me show you something. You'll like it. I know. Come on." He put out his hand for her. She took it.

They were walking up a marble stairway to the bedroom. The bedroom windows opened onto a tile balcony. Red camellias were planted in terra-cotta pots. They were walking into a huge dressing room. A sunken tub was in the bathroom. Everything was black marble. The faucets were gold. There were gold chandeliers hanging above them. Every wall had mirrors bordered by bulbs and gold. Lenny was standing in front of a closet.

"Pick something out. Go on. Walk in. Pink. You like pink? No. You like it darker. Yeah. Keep walking. Closet big as a tennis court. They got no taste, right? Looks like Vegas, right? You like red? No. Black. That's you. Here. Black silk." Lenny came out of the closet. He was holding an evening gown. "This your size? All you skinny broads wear the same size."

Lenny handed the dress to her. He stretched out on the bed. "Yeah. Let go of the towel. That's right. Only slower."

He was watching her. He lit a cigarette. His towel had come apart. He was holding something near his lap. It was a jewelry box.

"After you put that crap on your face, the paint, the lipstick, we'll pick out a little something nice for you. Phyllis won't need it. She's not coming back. Yeah." Lenny laughed. "Bernie and Phyllis are entertaining the Colombians by now. Give those boys from the jungle something to chew on. Don't look like that. You like diamonds? I know you like diamonds."

Lenny was stretched out on the bed. The bed belonged to Bernie and Phyllis but they weren't coming back. Lenny was holding a diamond necklace out to her. She wanted it more than she could remember wanting anything.

"I'll put it on you. Come here. Sit down. I won't touch you. Not unless you ask me. I can see you're all dressed up. Just sit near me. I'll do the clasp for you," Lenny offered.

She sat down. She could feel the stones around her throat, cool, individual, like the essence of something that lives in the night. Or something more ancient, part of the fabric of the night itself.

"Now you kiss me. Come on. You want to. I can tell. Kiss me. Know what this costs?" Lenny touched the necklace at her throat with his fingertips. He studied the stones. He left his fingers on her throat. "Sixty, seventy grand maybe. You can kiss me now."

She turned her face toward him. She opened her lips. Outside, the Santa Ana winds were startling, howling as if from a mouth. The air smelled of scorched lemons and oranges, of something delirious and intoxicated. When she closed her eyes, everything was blue.

She didn't see him at her noon meeting the next day or the day after. She thought, Well, that's it. I'll never see him again. She wasn't sorry. She got a manicure. She went to her psychiatrist. She began taking a steam bath after her aerobics class at the gym. She went Christmas shopping. She decided to give everyone crystal this year. She bought her daughter a white rabbit coat trimmed with blue fox. She was spending too much money. She didn't care.

It was Christmas Eve when the doorbell rang. There were carols on the radio. She was wearing a silk robe and smoking. She told Maria that she would answer the door.

"You promised never to come here." She was angry. "You promised to respect my life. To recognize my discrete borders."

"Discrete borders?" Lenny repeated. "I'm in serious trouble. Look at me. Can't you see there's something wrong? You look but you don't see."

There was nothing unusual about him. He was wearing blue jeans and a black leather jacket. He was carrying an overnight bag. She could see the motorcycle near the curb.

Maybe the Colombians had the red Ferrari. Maybe they were chewing on that now. She didn't ask him in.

"This is it," Lenny was saying. He brushed past her and walked into the living room. He was talking quickly. It would be months before she realized that his eyes and speech were wild from drugs. He was telling her what had happened in the desert, what the Colombians had done. She felt like she was being electrocuted, that her hair was standing on end. It occurred to her that it was a sensation so singular that she might come to enjoy it. There were small blue wounded sounds in the room now. She wondered if they were coming from her.

"I disappear in about five mintues." Lenny looked at her. "You coming?"

She thought about it. What she actually thought in this one moment was how Lenny had taken her to a restaurant, how she had started to translate the menu for him. How surprised she had been at his French.

"You don't get it, do you?" Lenny had laughed. "Saigon was a French city. You did business in French. You think Lenny crawled out from a rock? Yeah. I could tell you stories knock your socks off. Saigon. The women with their white parasols by the river. You Beverly Hills whores. You don't know."

"I can't come, no," she said finally. "I have a child."

"We take her," Lenny offered.

She shook her head, no. The room was going dark at the edges, she noticed. Like a field of blue asters, perhaps. Or ice when the sun strikes it. And how curious the blue becomes when clouds cross the sun, when the blue becomes broken, tawdry.

"I had plans for you. I was going to introduce you to some people. I should of met you fifteen years ago. I could of retired. Get me some ice," Lenny said. "Let's have a drink."

"We're in AA. Are you crazy?" She was annoyed.

"I need a drink. I need a fix. I need an automatic weapon. I need a plane," he said. He looked past her to the den. Maria was watching television and wrapping Christmas presents.

"You need a drink, too," Lenny said. "Don't even think about it. The phone. You're an accessory after the fact. You can go to jail. What about your kid then?"

They were standing in her living room. There was a noble pine tree near the fireplace. There were wrapped boxes beneath the branches. Maria asked in Spanish if she needed anything. She said not at the moment. Two glases with ice, that was all.

"Have a drink," Lenny said. "You can always go back to the meetings. They take you back. They don't mind. I do it all the time. All over the world. I've been doing it for ten years."

"I didn't know that," she said. It was almost impossible to talk. It occurred to her that her sanity was becoming intermittent, like a sudden stretch of intact road in an abandoned region. Or radio music, blatant after months of static.

"Give me the bottle. I'll pour you one. Don't look like that. You look like you're going down for the count. Here." Lenny handed the glass to her. She could smell the vodka. "Open your mouth, goddamn it."

She opened her mouth. She took a sip. Then she lit a cigarette.

"Wash the glass when I leave," Lenny said. "They can't prove shit. You don't know me. You were never anywhere. Nothing happened. You listening? You don't look like you're listening. You look like you're on tilt. Come on, baby. Listen to Daddy. That's good. Take another sip."

She took another sip. Lenny was standing near the door. "You're getting off easy, you know that? I ran out of time. I had plans for you," he was saying.

He was opening the door. "Some ride, huh? Did Daddy do like he said? Get you to the other side? You catch a glimpse? See what's there? I think you're starting to see. Can't say Lenny lied to you, right?"

She took another sip. "Right," she agreed. When this glass was finished she would pour another. When the bottle was empty, she would buy another.

Lenny closed the door. The night stayed outside. She was surprised. She opened her mouth but no sound came out. Instead, blue things flew in, pieces of glass or tin, or necklaces of blue diamonds, perhaps. The air was the blue of a pool when there are shadows, when clouds cross the turquoise surface, when you suspect something contagious is leaking, something camouflaged and disrupted. There is only this infected blue enormity elongating defiantly. The blue that knows you and where you live and it's never going to forget.

A Touch
of Autumn

IT IS A LATE THURSDAY AFTERNOON IN early autumn. Laurel Sloan drives west on Sunset Boulevard to UCLA where she teaches creative writing. Los Angeles is suddenly somehow a creature of amber and all the chilled yellow possibilities. It is the sort of gouged-open-and-washed-by-wind moment in which she contemplates the nature of poetry at the edge of the millennium. It is an afternoon so startling, so clear and sharp that she feels she could almost see the places where the poem intimates its morphology and desires. And the poem is about agitation and frailties, she decides, language and the betrayals of intimacy. Or perhaps none of this.

She parks her car and walks onto campus. The brick buildings are a deep rose in the fading afternoon. She hears the brass and drums of the marching band somewhere beyond the trees. The air smells of pine needles. The air feels like glass, absolute and dangerous, with subtle properties.

It occurs to her that this is the mirror where she dare not look.

It is nearly two hours before her class. She has arranged her day this way, to leave this punctuation of solitude where she might have a coffee and walk through the sculpture garden and consider the state of her sensibility as she prepares to turn forty.

Laurel Sloan feels, during these elongated Thursday early evenings, that she is still related to the person she was twenty years before. Standing in front of the campus gallery, she can believe that there is a continuity between the two versions of herself, the person she has somehow become and the young woman who contrived to spend entire days in the Louvre, convinced art was a necessity, like air. Or perhaps it was even more fundamental.

She had just graduated from Berkeley. She was twenty-one. She traveled across Europe wearing blue jeans and a Mexican poncho. She vowed that she would recognize no borders but those of aesthetic principles. She was a young woman who had to be in museums, had to sit on benches near the bronze of sculpture. Museums were a sanctuary. When she entered the space enclosing paintings, she felt the air was veiled and inviolate.

She thought it her duty to compare the blue and green of oceans and seas, the Pacific, the Mediterranean, the Aegean. Certainly these were the blue avenues that mattered. And these were the years when she always carried a notebook, thinking her impressions, her sketches with words were a kind of currency. Eventually, she would arrive in a region where they spoke of the ineluctable imperatives of the heart. In that city or port or capital, she would find a sense of familiarity that rendered explanation unnecessary. Here they spoke in the one dialect in which she was fluent.

She was a collector of landscapes and boulevards then,

the names of churches and the descriptions of miracles. Words opened like flowers, fragrant with implication. And there were the young men who played guitars, spent days in cafés, and were sometimes painters. They shared a common texture and vocabulary. They knew words were acts of inspiration and revolution. They knew words could alter the orbit of worlds. And when she remembers this era, it seems to be one unbroken late afternoon on a soft cliff above a tame harbor where she waited breathless for revelation.

Now, in the UCLA sculpture garden, dense with shadows and the residues from amber bulbs beyond the trees, casting their nets of refined clarities, she recalls her former self and pities it. She is filled with a monumental contempt. There was a red-haired man from Scotland who played guitar and sang songs about the brotherhood of man. She held a hat to collect coins for him in the Paris metro. This one event seems to her inconceivable. In this cool stalled moment, there is a scent of damp geraniums and anise, perhaps, something vague and squalid. As she recognizes this, she is struck by a thought, no, she is rocked and almost leveled by what feels as electric as inspiration. She thinks, *my best work is behind me.*

Simultaneously, she is aware of the press of another idea. Or perhaps it is not a separate architecture but rather an echo or shadow of the first. And it says, drink me. Of course, if she could have one single drink, one simple glass of Cazalla, say, she could be in the Spain of Lorca. Images would come to her as pigeons to bread crumbs in an afternoon plaza. She could be a lady of wrought-iron balconies and red camellias in the shadows of mountains and bullrings. She could know the harbor where the trade routes meet. She could hear the cathedral bells.

It would be the kind of early morning that seems to require a rendering in watercolor. The air would be informed by white African jasmine. It would be the sort of air where words find themselves effortlessly and create their own dynamic with precision and abandon. She could devise strategies of definition, entire theories of literature and algebras of resolutions in the solitary courtyard of a whitewashed study. She would work until nightfall, alone, with a bottle of wine and the company of almond and olive trees that have seen everything.

It occurs to her that one bottle of wine would be insufficient. A bottle of vodka would be better. With a bottle of Russian vodka, she could find some stance that would make turning forty alone endurable. With a glass in hand, her entire molecular structure would alter, becoming defined and edged. She could put a hand on her hip then and say, I am forty and alone and it's not what I thought, with my short French haircut and the walks I take in dusk hills with the city still and annointed by heat when the Santa Ana blows. My nights are always hot. That hasn't changed.

Laurel Sloan smiles. She would like to look into the infinite and treacherous face of night and say, so what if I chose this? I took entirely different vows. I courted destruction, oceans and narcotics, the dark side of the tropics, steaming, dense with creatures of inspired decadence. I was purified by intensity. I demanded an infinity of green and occasionally I got it.

If she had a drink, she could face the night and stare it down. It is only a temptation, after all, only damp corridors haunted by plumeria where we calibrate the years with our rage. And what is there to fear? It is only death or failure or some blue agony that burns.

Laurel Sloan would like to say this, to say it is only me, after all, finally possessing this sensibility, this sudden autumnal island behind my forehead, with its undamaged interiors, its green bridges and praying green mouths. Of course, if she could drink again, then images and rhythms would be enough. They would sustain her. She can remember when she was willing to live or die for a single stanza, one glimpse of a dissected moment infected by moon. Such a singular moment required vodka, which seemed to contain some celestial impulse made liquid and manifest, some corruption of the elements she had perversely come to crave.

It is later, after the cafés above harbors where she sat with a notebook, describing the quality of light and the sound of bells. It was after the museums and the men who were painters. She became convinced that sensibility was structural.

It was autumn in Maui, in a tropical variation of fall, in suggestion and in a slight moistening in the perpetual damp and green. She lived in a shack on a river without a name in a jungle near Hana. The edges were red ginger. The afternoons seemed unborn, humid between Kona storms. The heat seemed ancient. History and interpretation meant nothing. Here there were only the nuances of languid, the postures of silence, wind in palms, and the restless sky struggling for definition and release. The rain. The wind. The sky at the edge of a profound rearrangement. The elongated afternoon with its illusionary borders of red ginger and the scent of kerosene and some vestigial red assertion.

Laurel Sloan recognizes that the lies which informed her life were abstract and impermanent. Her lover, Derek, was like that, abstract and impermanent. He could be anyone. He was a sketch for a human being. There wasn't enough detail. In such a region, omissions became significant. Form was revealed by the details that accumulated like weeds or dust or baskets of laundry. Or the sculpture of Gordon's vodka bottles six feet high behind the shack where they lived. Here the landscape spoke of its disease through untarnished lips. The landscape was an oracle.

Laurel Sloan is surprised, standing now in the glassy ambered air of UCLA in autumn in early evening, how her sadness seems restrained, almost elegant. Above her, the sunset is quick and decisive. We light the candle, she thinks, and we blow the candle out.

There is something more about candles, the shack she shared with Derek, the jungle in autumn. She is saying they have no propane, no batteries, no food. Derek is playing a Doors song on his guitar. Derek is drinking from a bottle slowly, as if it weren't that important, was an afterthought, really, a minor detail. He is undisturbed. They still have vodka.

"But we have no light," Laurel persists. This seems somehow significant. They cannot get to the highway or the country store. It might be across an ocean. They have been out of cigarettes for two days.

"We've got candles," Derek tells her. He is staring out the mesh that is nailed to the wood. He is looking past the lanai at the river. He is thirty-six.

"One candle," Laurel is saying, suddenly frightened.

Derek doesn't say anything. She doesn't want to know what he is thinking or what he sees in the river.

"What happens when the candle is gone?" Laurel experiences a confusion that feels vast. She thinks of the Pacific at night, that stretch of ocean below the cliffs where she sometimes goes, where the water turns an agitated black that looks like malignant stone.

"There are stars," Derek says.

"And if it rains?" Laurel is breathless. She waits a long time.

Finally Derek says, "Then there are no stars." He is looking at the river.

"What will we do if there are no stars? If it rains? And we have no light?" Laurel is holding a flashlight that contains dead batteries. She refuses to remove them. She thinks if she presses the metal, if she somehow warms it with the heat from her body, it will come to life.

"Then we'll just look into each other's eyes," Derek says. It is not an invitation.

Laurel Sloan is holding a useless flashlight. She is living on a river without electricity, at the end of eight miles of illegal dirt road. They have no propane, food, or batteries. It occurs to her that there is something terribly wrong with her life. It has to do with the flashlight and with Derek and looking into his eyes. She is afraid. She knows they are empty, they are hollow, they are screens where images are painted. But nothing gets in.

Now it is past sunset. She is standing in the sculpture garden. There is a touch of wind. She feels as if she is standing in a sudden emotional clearing, striking and definitive. A string of moments are exhibiting themselves as if the winds of autumn had a congruency in the soul.

She remembers Northern California. It was a spicy yellow autumn, punched out and alive. She was driving the car she would later crash. It was after Maui. She was driving the car the only way she thought possible, too fast, with a bottle of vodka in a brown paper bag on the front seat. It sat next to her. It was one of her friends, after all. She was playing Dylan with the volume turned all the way up. She had a quarter of an ounce of cocaine folded in plastic in her jacket pocket. She touched it as she drove. It was her talisman from the god she understood. She worshipped and adored it.

In her purse, she carried a silver pill box with pain medications and tranquilizers. A cigarette package bounced across the dashboard. There were several joints in it, a chunk of black hash and a small ash-colored ball of opium.

In the glove compartment was a locked jewlery box. It had once played music when the lid was lifted but now it was silent. Laurel Sloan had removed the mechanism to create more space for her paraphernalia. The locked box contained a hash pipe, cigarette papers, a plastic bottle filled with rubbing alcohol, a lighter, two books of matches, a soup spoon with her initials engraved in silver flowers along the handle, an envelope with ten one hundred dollar bills, balls of cotton in a plastic bag, a long thin red rubber cord and several disposable syringes. They were designed to be disposable but she used them for weeks. That was a detail she chose not to think about.

Laurel Sloan rarely left her house with less than this. These were the minimum chemicals that she required to exist on this hostile planet. She could not hold a pen without these substances. She could not wake up or go to sleep, take a plane, or make a telephone call without them. She needed these things to get dressed, to brush her teeth and walk to her car. She could not possibly operate her automobile without these chemicals. She recognized that they were part of her life the way her lipstick was, her license and car keys. They were a fact of life she simply took for granted.

It was a day of startling blue and yellow. She was smoking a cigarette and drinking vodka from the bottle. It was breakfast. She was thinking that there were elements of luck in all things, geography, anatomy, the ritual astonishment of seasons. She was driving the highway to Bodega Bay at eighty miles an hour, winding through Queen Anne's lace and asters embroidering the sides of the road above the Russian River. And she suddenly realized that this moment above the Russian River would happen only once, like birth and death.

This is why we buy souvenirs, she recognized, why we send postcards. This is why we give our daughters the names of flowers, Iris, Hyacinth, Rose.

She stopped her car. She walked to a cliff with its determined blue scratchings of waves below and she stood in the rising breeze and wept for the daughter she did not have and would probably never have. Then she threw her drugs into the violent wind of afternoon. She had glimpsed the essence, the fragile structure that bound the irrefutable moments one to another. These were the clarities that would later be called a life or history. She considered the implications of this in a kind of torment or rapture. By midnight, in Berkeley, she had purchased more chemicals in glass bottles and plastic bags and she was drinking.

Now it is UCLA at night. And Laurel Sloan has not had a drink in almost three years. She is walking across a lawn between brick buildings on paths in an air that seems composed of the cold yellow dangers. An air that has known the intrigue of metals, perhaps, and witnessed angry stars or been employed in ambiguous rituals. She is thinking that her arrested adolescence and squandered youth left her unprepared for this, her fortieth year, when the poetry she once wrote seems remote and soiled.

What was it really, Laurel Sloan thinks, all that scratching and garish personal mutilation? All that hoarded solitude guarded and starved for across two decades of substandard housing? It was a tiny aberration, weightless, invisible like poison gas. It was like a virulent obsolete fever one knows by footnotes and rumor. Then it left, abandoning her in a truncated autumn in a brutal year.

Laurel Sloan is walking through the sculpture garden past a huge woman and then some sort of enormous orifice.

This is what we are, she thinks, permanent openings, cavities where the wind riots. She glances at a group of low metal pieces that have been installed beneath trees. They look like some version of extraterrestrials. Whatever you have come here for, you will encounter only disappointment, she thinks.

She stands in front of a Rodin without a head. It is bronze and moss, and how green it looks, as if becoming organic. And further, on the lawn, in puddles of darkness, sculptures lay in the illumination of small lamps. They look like they assembled themselves.

Laurel stands in the pastel glow from strips of soft neon. There are humanoid figures in the grass, some missing limbs or skulls. They are attached to blocks of cement like prisoners in a perpetual night.

Laurel Sloan finds herself staring at a sculpture that looks as if it had been dropped from above and allowed to fall into mute pieces. We are bisected, she thinks, we are elongated, we are magnified. We sit in fountains spurting water from too many orifices. We put the typewriter on the floor under the dining room table and live there. We are safe with the wood over our heads. We sit there for eleven days and nights, consecutively, making holes in the veins of our arms and legs. We write poems in blood. We think we are justified. Our arms are infected. We suspect we are not as God intended. We have a profusion of cavities. Our gender is monumental. Isn't that what our sculpture tells us? We are appetite without skulls. We are amputated. We have children without husbands. We have our babies completely alone like a renegade species. We have no tribes or totems. We have no rituals of solace. When we are born or when we die no one lights candles. No one can remember the litanies, the words to summon and amuse the gods. We live alone. We are celibate for decades. We have been dropped to earth and deserted. Perhaps we are music. Someone listened to us fall. Perhaps we are a degraded form of rain.

She is standing in front of an angular configuration that might be a dog from another and more affectionate world. Above, the sky is pinching out another meek night blue horizon. The sculptures seem to have shells. Perhaps they are prophetic, Laurel is thinking. They are armored, as if already sensing radiation and nuclear winter and evolving a protection of bronze.

It occurs to her that the lawn is littered with autopsies under a half moon. Perhaps these figures of tortured metal tell us we are no longer of this world. We are ruins. We have the serenity of the utterly defeated, that which surrenders to the stasis of perpetual geometry. This is all there is, this cemetery of distortion and its hideous implications.

Laurel Sloan imagines that her life will always be like these acres of agitated solitude or some others, also empty and repetitive with unanswered longings. She will always feel alternatively drowned and immolated. In Los Angeles or Maui or Bodega Bay, she will walk night hills with the moon unusually white and still and cool and nothing will sustain her. There will be a solitude so dimensional and seamless she will feel nautical, buried beneath blue waters. That and the craving for cocaine which is permanent. They will bury her with it.

Laurel Sloan realizes that she wants to go to the Faculty Center. She is already walking in that direction, down stairs, across rectangular courtyards. She desires this sudden destination absolutely, inside, where she is turning to water. She will get one coffee in the lounge downstairs. She will sip coffee while the others drink wine. What is one negligible temptation, after all, when one considers the nature of our sculpture, with the doomed and mutated legions we invent for ourselves? We are a refugee species lacking even ordinary symmetry. We are mutilated. Nothing rises from ash. This earth is hell and the months of our unbearable incarnations unlock one upon another.

She is crossing a courtyard on a diagonal cement path. She is walking quickly. She is thinking that she has lost some vital connection with her life, with all that is inviolate, spontaneous, and assured. Perhaps it was lost by chance, an accident, unusually heavy traffic. Perhaps it is something we knew but forget, like footsteps on a locked boulevard in a warm afternoon in autumn in a region on the border between death and the Mardi Gras. Isn't that where we live, before the exile and eventual autopsy? There is only the line, after all, that frontier between a street party and a terminal disease. Always we are standing at a window, looking down at our lives, our lies, the ruins of evening and seasons, this one and all others.

She is near the Faculty Center. She can sense the way wood softens when it encloses rooms in which wine is being poured. She thinks of the dining room where bottles are set near a piano on a wooden bar. Candles are lit in front of them like an altar. You can know God with your mouth. There are no more apprenticeships. You don't need instruction from the old men. There are no years of memorization.

Laurel Sloan imagines the lounge. She will sit on a blue couch in front of the fireplace. It is autumn, after all, the season of wood and glass. And in that room, the bottles behind the bar are set on glass shelves like artifacts.

She is quickening her pace. There is no sound worth noting in the universe, only her boots on cement. Her life has left without her, has deserted her, but she can still sit in the lounge before her seven o'clock class. She is wondering what she missed in this desperate hallucination. A subtle angular refinement, perhaps? A polished ornament or a chance remark?

Then, suddenly, the world divests itself of subterfuge. If she can just sit at the bar where the clarities are distilled, she could answer these and all other questions. She envisions the label on a vodka bottle, with the script insistent as a postcard from Kauai. Or a medieval document, an illumination imposed upon the pagan. If she could just sit near the bar where definition is by fifths and quarts, she could know the white lyricism of liquid measurement.

"Ms. Sloan?" a voice in the almost darkness asks. People are coming out of the autumn night like severed foliage, she is thinking, like leaves falling. They blow in your face.

"Yes?" It is the yes when her name is called in art galleries, parking lots, and department stores. The nurse with your blood workup. Always we are saying yes to a stranger and turning toward the sudden conjunction of our destinies, half-expecting a stilleto, half-expecting a rose. It is autumn in Los Angeles. It is a plague year. It is some time near the millennium. It could be anything.

"I wanted to tell you how much your class means to me. You're a model for me." It is a student apparently, not leaves with miniature mouths wearing camouflage and carrying Uzis. It is not immediate disaster, after all, but a woman with long red earrings and wild hair.

"Yes?" Laurel Sloan repeats. She says this mechanically, impatiently. What she wants to say is, get out of my way. I need a drink.

"You're proof a person can come out the other side," this wild haired student is telling her with a trembling voice.

Laurel Sloan is drawn to the red earrings. They are extravagant, like an ornament in the wind. This is an artifact from a forest people. She is staring at the earrings. It is more than one pair, she realizes. This young woman has

pierced her ear several times and placed various configurations of glass and tin in each hole. Laurel knows it is the
fashion. Still, she is repelled.

The wind is blowing. Soon her class will begin. She will
ride the elevator to the third floor of Bunche Hall where
sixteen students will be sitting at a rectangular conference
table with poems and pieces of short prose. Sixteen candles
in the unremitting waste, in the malevolent clutter we call
cities and fill with potent debris. Our ruins are radioactive.
They have half-lives larger than empires or emptiness itself.
And somewhere, a bit player is saying, look at history. It's
always been brutal. Have a drink, someone is always saying.
Have a few. And soon it will be too late for her to have
even one.

"How do you do it?" this student with the profusion of
punctures in her ears is asking. Her name is Melissa, Laurel
Sloan remembers. Melissa is saying, "Until you told me a
writer needs the stamina of a channel swimmer and the
faith of a fanatic, I was lost. You've changed my life."

Laurel Sloan considers the possibility that this is a ritual
of degradation. Here her tawdry fantasies are revealed.
They are embodied by people Central Casting sent. She is
standing in the deepening dark and cold a few yards from
the Faculty Center. Between her and the room with the
vodka is a gulf in which reside the enormities, the accidents,
the random atrocities and also the sudden avenues of
inexplicable grace. Here we are stripped to bone, that's how
hard and pointed and beyond flesh we have become. We
are spine and marrow and purpose, the core that survives
centuries, glistening, washed by moon and night and one
insolent autumn after another. Here we are haunted. It is
a sea of broken hours. Here we discover fire. We burn one
another. Eventually, somewhere on the banks of a dusk

river, a prayer is offered in our name, a candle lit and the killing season shifts.

"Can I walk with you?" Melissa asks.

So, we're walking. So, at least that's settled. Walking through the enormities that are always there in the wind annointed plateau, in the inexhaustible mesas of autumn where we live.

"They say you don't drink anymore. Is that true?" Melissa asks.

"Yes," Laurel Sloan says, "it's true." The days are lit by our energy, our incarnations. We are nailed between horizons, moment upon moment. There is the narrative of waves, the clouds, somewhere a full moon and stars with their lucid confederations.

"You're fantastic," this student almost whispers. Her hand has gone to her throat.

Last night, in her bath, it suddenly occurred to Laurel that the vein in her right arm was wide and clean enough to land a 747 on. She held her arm up to the light, admiring the substantiality of her vein, how it had contrived to rise to the surface again after years where it had disappeared, collapsed from abuse. Her vein said, I am Lazarus. Kiss me with metal.

"I take certain actions on a daily basis. Meditation, prayer, AA meetings," Laurel Sloan begins. She is thinking that sensibility is a set of disciplines. That is the way we make ourselves more attractive to God. She is telling this student about the long walks she takes in the hills. She is thinking that there is also the luck of the draw. And how sometimes the foliage itself speaks in a clairvoyant dialect.

In between we fence hell, Laurel Sloan is thinking. We fence it and later there will be small plots, farms, a town or two. These are the gestures, the posts we drive into the rock to string the nets on. These are the tangible expressions. We erect grids where there is nothing.

Sixteen young writers wait at a conference table. They are holding invisible candles. We touch them with flame. We hike the ridge whether we feel like it or not, every day. There are no exceptions. We fall to our knees every morning. We promise to divest ourselves of our manias, even the beloved ones. If we must embrace silence, then we will be mute. There are only the gestures and their resonances. There are only these arabesques across glass.

"I might have a problem with cocaine," Melissa softly confesses.

Laurel is thinking, then drive yourself mad and die. Have a heart attack. Go to prison. Crash your car. Take forays into the plague zone. Consort with men who inject drugs. Why bother me? We have nothing in common. We are both sentient beings on the third planet from the sun, that is all. Laurel opens her mouth. She says, "I'll take you to a meeting."

They are walking across a courtyard where the brick seems embued with some rare essence of rose. They are riding the elevator to the third floor of Bunche Hall. On the other side of the building, below, the sculpture garden lays under the half moon with its bisected bodies in their limbo of night. There, below, in the irradiated cemetery are the shattered men and exaggerated women, the atrocities that foretell us.

Now they are walking along the outer terrace of the building. Palms push up from below, somehow asserting a continuity between divisions, even where the gulf is defiant. She is thinking it is possible that there is a continuum between who she was in Majorca in 1971 and now, between the girl in the café in Palma talking about Lorca and now. She is still reading Lorca. Sensibility is structural. And everywhere there are rivers where churches and temples surrender their temporary form and lay down as ruins, settled into the peace of uncorrupted geometry, the dreams of stone.

It is fall. It is always fall, Laurel Sloan is thinking. And we are sober. We have even stopped smoking. Maybe we can say what we've been thinking all along. Jim Morrison is dead. The boys with their guitars and vans are gone. The guitars are gone and the music. Insane and broken people sleep in the streets. They wear rags. Their bare feet are black. They cough. Their bones show. They look as if they assembled themselves. Some carry plague. We don't know this country or what it's become. We are forty and alone. It is the resurrection of glass. And we all have a touch of autumn, perhaps, like an X-ray with a touch of shadow on the lung.

TEMPORARY

LIGHT

IT IS EARLY IN DECEMBER. SUZANNE COOPER drives down Wilshire Boulevard through Beverly Hills and the city is not as she knew it. Overnight, wide red ribbons have been entwined around street lamps, there is simulated snow and frost in shop windows, and legions of slaughtered pines are everywhere decorated and displayed. It is as if the earth had suddenly divested itself of the ordinary and revealed its pagan interior. Or perhaps the world had without warning gone mad, she decides, garish red and green and silver like a bleeding forest under moonlight. This is a landscape of dangerous wounds and corrupted vegetation.

At a traffic light she finds herself staring at a Santa Claus with a sleigh of reindeer strung on wires across the intersection. Everywhere, strands of light bulbs rise into the air. Even the sky seems delirious and experimental. It is the winter of the wild surprise. The old regime does not apply. Have a drink, the voice in her head says.

It is Suzanne Cooper's second sober Christmas. She has learned to recognize the voice of her illness, the demonic chorus it employs and the genius motivating its attempts to destroy her. The voice could be articulate, brilliant, and seductive. It is the disaster that never sleeps.

I have a killer disease that wants me dead, she remembers. I have a daily reprieve based on the maintenance of my spiritual life. She repeats the slogans she has memorized in Alcoholics Anonymous, the banalities designed to provide a rudimentary form of counterattack against the onslaught of her alcoholism. It is like a chess game played by two computers to a series of perpetual stalemates. She is always black and on the defensive. Her sickness is aggressive and white, the color of vodka, gin, and wine.

At the next stop sign, she glances into a shop window dense with a red-and-green geometric motif. Mirrors amplify the distortion. Mannequin elves offer demented smiles. They look as if they have taken enormous doses of mescaline.

You're pathetic, the voice says, with your tiny arsenal, your squalid weaponry. And it won't be enough, not nearly. Consider the thin air beneath you. You have no net. You will fall and shatter and your blood run. One small glass of eggnog with a drop of brandy. No one will know.

Suzanne Cooper turns her car into the monumental parking structure beneath the Beverly Center. This year she is shopping early. Last Christmas she was in the hospital. This year will be different. This year she will see her children. Stephanie and Mark will spend Christmas Eve and Christmas Day with her. This has become her imperative, the irrefutable meaning of her present life. Her actions derive from the fact of Christmas. It has become the spine of her world, the anatomy she accepts as necessary.

In a boutique on the sixth level of the mall, yard-square

aluminum representations of snowflakes sway above her head. She wonders if each one is in fact different and unique from the others. "Jingle Bells" plays relentlessly, asserting itself from unseen speakers. The voice in her head substitutes the word "martini" for jingle bells. "Mar-ti-ni, mar-ti-ni, mar-ti-ni to-day," the voice intones tirelessly as she lifts scarves and sweaters and cannot focus her eyes. She is conscious of the sharp-edged metallic snowflakes just above her. She is holding clothing between her fingers, bolts of fabric, some square, others vertical. She feels confused, suddenly hot, as if she has been struck with a virulent flu. Then she walks out of the store.

On a higher level of the mall, Suzanne finds herself standing in a shop excessive with Christmas manifestations. Six tall trees straddle stacks of wrapped and ribboned gifts. A colossal wreath is suspended from the ceiling. The walls glow with strings of gold lights. This is not Christmas as Suzanne Cooper remembers it.

Last year she did not even send Christmas cards. She was only one month sober. She could barely walk the hospital corridors. It seemed that there had been rain and carolers had come, schoolchildren wearing bells. She had closed the door.

It occurs to her that the other Christmasses of her life are partial memories, images in a blackout, something like a village glimpsed in a blizzard. There are the meals she burned, the gifts she forgot to wrap or send. The line in the post office was offensive and boring, she thought as she drank from a bottle stashed in her car. She would return later, when the line was smaller, but of course she didn't, drove to Malibu instead and crashed the car. She is thinking of the Malibu sheriff's station and the ambulance on the Pacific Coast Highway as she stands beneath a gigantic wreath suspended from the ceiling. Then, somehow, she buys her first gifts of the season.

Even as the packages are being wrapped, the dark blue velvet dress with a white lace collar for Stephanie and a red-and-green sweater with a border of reindeer for Mark, a discreet implication of Christmas adorning the area near the shoulders, Suzanne feels dissatisfied. The wrapping paper is red embossed with green trees and the red seems to glare challengingly. She is conscious of the voices in her head complaining, mimicking her children. "Oh, another dress," the condemning voice of Stephanie says, allowing herself the restrained disappointment of understatement. In the silence, Stephanie would not have to say, how dull, how could you? It's riding pants I long for.

"There are reindeer on here," the representation of Mark accuses, using the inflections of mock astonishment. "Mother, I can't wear reindeer," the approximation of Mark tells her, his voice soft like his father, the phrasing that of a lecture.

In their eyes she is something like a slow child to be tutored. She realizes they do not expect much from her, she of the ruined dinners and automobiles and hospitals. She of the diminished capacities. And she recognizes that their estimation is similar to her mother's. Somehow she has managed to replicate that which she most loathes.

And somewhere, always near, her mother Candace, her tone sharp and offended, says, "Put that down, dear. You can't afford it. They won't appreciate it. They never do. How could they, with that breeding? I told you, put that back." It occurs to Suzanne that she is trembling. She reaches out her hands for the packages, the red that glares dangerously, and walks out of the extravagantly wreathed store. For a moment, she experiences a sense of triumph.

She has at last purchased something. Suzanne feels as if

she has finally drawn blood in the consumer hunting season. She enters a stationery store. A wordless version of "Jingle Bells" descends from the wall and ceiling speakers like an invisible flock of tiny, menacing birds. "Mar-ti-ni, mar-tin-i, mar-tin-i to-day." Then she begins to study the boxes of Christmas cards. She considers her potential selections methodically, working her way first vertically and then horizontally across the rows.

Suzanne Cooper weighs the resonances of the cards, not merely the issue of style and content, typeface and graphics, but the more elusive fundamental essence. There are subtleties. She rules out snow scenes in any guise. This is California and it would be, after all, contrived. Santa Claus in any form is too childish and cute. The elves are unspeakable. Birds of peace are a possibility. And flowers and bells and cards from nonprofit agenices. There is also the matter of recycled paper. She stacks her first round of potential selections in a pile near the counter. The stack rises beside the cash register.

Suzanne Cooper considers the implications of "Merry Christmas" versus "Joy," and the distinctions implicit in "Season's Greetings" and "Happy Holidays." The voice in her head objects to all of her selections. Too religious, it chides her. Too flamboyant, it comments, voice stern. Suzanne feels inadequate. She experiences a sudden sense of rage that takes her breath away.

Of course, "Merry Christmas" is too specific. What if one doesn't celebrate Christmas? What if one isn't merry, has just gone through a divorce, a suicide, or drug overdose in the family? Or a malignant biopsy, a touch of cancer perhaps? What if one is an alcoholic and has been removed from her family and then banished to a small apartment in Santa Monica? Was there a card appropriate to her circumstances?

She finds herself holding a box offering "Joy" in pastels. The motif is simultaneously intimidating and seductive, avant-garde in a terrifying way. It could mean anything, this "Joy," even things she could not articulate or control. Finally, Suzanne decides to buy three boxes of "Season's Greetings." These permutations seem manageable. Still, she feels little confidence as she departs from the store.

On the top level of the mall, in a kind of enclosure past the movie theaters that remind her of a Greyhound bus station in a depressed city, Suzanne Cooper drinks a café au lait and wishes that she could smoke again. If she had a cigarette, she could make more accurate assessments in her shopping, she would be calmer and more assured. Her brain and hand–eye coordination would be vastly improved. She watches someone smoking near her and it occurs to her that if she smoked, she would look glamorous and capable. Store clerks would not dare defraud her. Smoke a cigarette, just one, the voice in her head says. It's Christmas. You can have one.

Suzanne turns her attention to the Christmas cards she has just selected. She views the cards as if they were the distillation of her personality, the highest tangible achievement of her sensibility. She notices that the card approximates a kind of typewriter script and duplicates the phrase "Season's Greetings" relentlessly, as if struck by a mental illness or a form of repetitive nervous disorder. She feels repelled and somehow betrayed. There is a lack of authenticity about the card that profoundly saddens her. She recognizes that she would not wish to receive such a card.

She walks to a Mrs. Field's Cookies bordering the eating enclosure and purchases four large white chocolate with macadamia nut cookies. She eats two of them, quickly, and immediately feels better. This year she will manage the ritual of Christmas, with all its garish atrocities and bizarre paraphernalia. These pathetic rituals are our cumulative definition, she thinks, concurrently agitated and resigned.

This year she will decorate a Christmas tree and hang a wreath of noble pine on her front door. She will bake cookies shaped like Christmas trees. She will cover them with green sugar that resembles bits of glass. She has practiced the recipe already. She has told Stephanie about their striking stained-glass appearance. Stephanie, with polite silence accentuating her lack of enthusiasm, has reluctantly agreed to participate. They will wear matching white aprons Suzanne has purchased just for this activity. She has imbued the baking activity with spiritual qualities that require special garments like vestments. They will bake cookies together and this action will resonate and subtly bond them. She will duplicate the winter landscape with a version of her own, green and white, like a form of voodoo, or the manifestation of a powerful concurrency.

Suzanne realizes that the stained-glass cookie project has attained an almost mystical significance for her. She wants her entire life filled with tangible manifestations of the calming and predictable. Her personal evolution has been characterized by what she now views as fierce years of barbarism. Her own private ice ages, so to speak, her centuries of retrograde behavior and perception. Now she is committed to the larger traditional demarcations. Events such as Christmas have been clarified and redeemed. She no longer views them as acts of indifferent hypocrisy but rather as collective cultural statements of faith.

She eats another white chocolate and macadamia nut cookie and reviews this knowledge of personal evolution with herself. It occurs to her that she might be preparing for an oral exam in a subject in which she is not comfortable and has merely memorized themes. She glares at the Christmas cards with their leaden assertion of greetings and the words seem to leave the page, to somehow retreat and pale.

"I don't drink anymore," she told Candace. It was the previous summer. She had taken her mother out for lunch. It was July. They sat in the Polo Lounge at the Beverly Hills Hotel. The air seemed somehow yellow and pink, tropical but tamed and elegant. She had taken Candace out of the institution on a half-day pass.

"But you can have one glass of wine with your mother. Of course you can," Candace chided her. Her mother was dressed entirely in pink, a pink Chanel suit and hat and silk scarf. Even the diamonds on her brooch and rings seemed pink in the filtered and restrained midafternoon light. Such a sweet lady, a passing stranger might think. Candace ordered a scotch on the rocks. She drank it quickly and signaled with a diamond-tiered hand for another.

"Have a drink with your mother," Candace ordered. Her voice was fueled with rage. Her face was flushed. Even her eyes looked pink. Her eyes were the pink of certain predatory birds, or perhaps more distinctly reptilian like chameleons. Have a drink with your mother, you must, the voice within her announced.

"You're contemptible," Candace decided, drinking with exaggerated relish and ordering another. She wore pink lipstick. Even the scotch in her glass looked pink.

"What kind of celebration is this?" Candace demanded. "You always disappoint me. No"—she paused, then faced her daughter—"you betray me. That is a constant."

Candace pushed her chair away from the table. She stood up, unsteady. She pointed a finger encased with diamonds at her. Her voice was loud now. "You always lie to me,"

Candace shouted. She was still holding her scotch glass. She studied the glass in her hand as if she was uncertain what the object was. Then she threw it in Suzanne's face.

Suzanne had been startled by the liquor, how cool it was, how familiar the scent. She closed her eyes then, the better to breathe it in.

Later, she had telephoned her former husband. She told Jake that she had been forced to call the hospital. Candace had been taken from the Polo Lounge in an ambulance.

"Naturally," Jake had said distantly, as if adjusting something while they spoke, a shoelace, perhaps, or the television, the newspaper, the skirt of a new woman, or jogging shoes. "She's mentally ill."

"I didn't drink," Suzanne had told her former husband.

"Why would you?" Jake had answered, surprised, as if the thought had never occurred to him. "You don't drink anymore."

He made it sound as if she had a minor infection and had received the appropriate antibiotic and now it was over, done with, part of her ancient history, less than a footnote. It was remote to him because she was no longer important. He had filed for divorce while she was still in the hospital. The outcome of her hospitalization did not matter to him. She could drink herself to death or remain abstinent, in either event he was finished with her. He had kept the house in Beverly Hills and the children remained with him. She had gone from the hospital to a one-bedroom apartment in Santa Monica. She had been banished. It had never occurred to her that this might happen. It had been, literally, unthinkable.

■   ■   ■

Suzanne Cooper drives from the Beverly Center shopping mall west toward the ocean. The landscape is manicured and swept clean, a perpetual warm winter of bougainvillea and poinsettia on sunny hillsides above the loitering Pacific. On impulse, she parks her car on the bluffs above Santa Monica Bay. It occurs to her, suddenly, that there are certain moments and angles that are almost bearable. There are white sailboats on the bay. The water seems anemic and dazed. Waves break slowly and without malice. The Pacific is simply a fact for her, a blue beyond judgment, taken for granted. A sense of definition asserts itself at the periphery of her awareness. She realizes that nuances and the blue increments will come later, if at all.

She finds it necessary to reiterate the central facts of her existence, that she is thirty-seven years old, the divorced wife of Jake, the mother of Stephanie and Mark. She is a sober member of Alcoholics Anonymous. She doesn't drink anymore, ever. This year her children will spend Christmas Eve and Christmas Day with her. She will not fall asleep with a lit cigarette burning in an ashtray or pass out in the garden with her nightgown on. She no longer smokes and she no longer has a garden. She is reliable now. Even Jake's attorney has finally agreed to accept, provisionally, this concept. Yes, she is becoming the sort of woman who puts the appropriate change into parking meters and mails her Christmas cards on time. She is becoming the sort of woman one could exile to an apartment in Santa Monica knowing that she would accept it with quiet dignity. She is the sort of woman one could banish with little expense.

Suzanne Cooper walks along the Santa Monica cliffs feeling oddly hollow, as if her bones are merely a grid, a suggestion for an armature not yet developed. She walks into a gift shop bizarre with decorations, its shelves flaunting color and pyramids of oddities she can barely decipher. She holds a plastic ashtray with a picture of the Santa Monica Bay, overly representational, the water is never that shade of ineffable blue anymore. *"Feliz Navidad"* is written in an offensive red script across the exaggerated too-green shoreline. Her hand feels soiled.

You need a drink, her voice reminds her. It is a patient voice. No one will know, it tells her. They don't care anyway. Drunk or sober, they have no use for you. One Bloody Mary. It won't kill you. 'Tis the season. 'Tis the season to be jolly. And you won't be surprising anyone. They expect it. They expect you to slip. They'll forgive you. You can always go back to AA after the holidays, in January, when the world turns dull and normal.

As she walks to her car, the light sea breeze brushes her body and she feels insubstantial, as if she might blow away. Then she drives to her noon AA meeting. She raises her hand and is called on to share. She wants to tell them how she has been exiled to an apartment in Santa Monica but she does not. Instead, she talks about her difficulty selecting the absolutely perfect Christmas card. Everyone laughs sympathetically. The women nod their heads with recognition. But she does not tell them that Stephanie and Mark will be spending Christmas with her. She imagines her children climbing the stairs to her apartment with their sleeping bags, their eyes expertly adjusting to her limited perimeters. Stephanie and Mark exchanging glances that say, Look at her minuscule domain. She is even less than we thought.

Suzanne Cooper spends her alloted three minutes making a humorous anecdote of her inability to choose a Christmas card that will solve all of her problems. She does not mention the fact that Stephanie and Mark will be spending Christmas with her under duress. They have both telephoned, separately, asking to be released from this obligation. Jake is going skiing in Aspen with his current girlfriend, the redhead with the free concert tickets. The one who took them to David Bowie and U2. Jake had suddenly become a skier. He had discovered rock and roll. He can take airplanes now, his fear of plane crashes has disappeared. It is as if her miniaturization has somehow enlarged him. This is what Suzanne is actually thinking while she talks about Christmas shopping. When she finishes, she glances at the women she has successfully deceived. Quite unexpectedly, she realizes that she detests them all.

That night the wind becomes agitated and cold. There is a storm and then, almost immediately, another. It rains for the next two weeks. The night wind seems increasingly personal and specific. She prepares her apartment for the arrival of her children who do not want to be there. She has never before managed the literal details of Christmas by herself. She ties a Christmas tree to the roof of her car and drives with branches splayed across the windshield. She drags the tree up the stairs to her apartment as it rains. She decorates it with new ornaments. The hand-sewn sequined snowflakes her grandmother made remain with Jake and the children. Her tree seems pathetic in comparison, deformed like a kind of dwarf, something small enough for her to carry, and adorned with the standard and ordinary. She tries to erase her sense of humiliation about the tree as she hangs a wreath on her front door. She stockpiles cookie-baking ingredients.

It rains the night of her children's Christmas pageant. It has been decided that she will pick them up after their performance. Jake's attorney has relented and she will be allowed to be with her children in an automobile for the first time in years. Then she will take them to her tiny dominion, which they will translate into something squalid. They will be excessively polite with her. Their eyes will be angry and bored.

She is imagining her children's eyes as she parks her car in the school parking lot. She is struck by the force of the wind as she walks. The sudden cutting press of it seems more than a function of literal climate. It seems to be a revelation of some brutal interior.

She finds a seat in the school auditorium. A seat for one. There is a moment of darkness and then the lights come on, soft and pink and radiant, as if there had been a kind of clarification. The pageant unfolds gracefully. The program is titled *Fiesta de las Luces*. Children rush across the darkened stage holding flashlights. They are comets. They are comets in the void or perhaps they are meant to represent random pulses of inspiration. Suzanne considers this, breathlessly. A child with a white robe speaks into a microphone, explaining that it is not only Christmas and Hanukkah, but a rare conjunction of planets and calendars makes this also the Hindu celebration of Ramadan and the African festival of Kwanza.

Suzanne Cooper is stunned by the implications of this universal recognition of light. Children appear and sing a Christmas carol in Spanish and then a chant in an African dialect. An older boy appears and recites passages from Genesis and the Upanishads. Suzanne is struck by the thought that somewhere, candles are being put into boats and they are gliding across unpronounceable rivers. Stephanie appears and stands in a circle with five other girls, singing a lullaby about stars in winter. The stage fills with children wearing African masks and others dancing like dervishes.

It occurs to her that this is her first Christmas pageant. Last year she was in the hospital. Before that, each year by this time she was drunk. Now she is sober and the spectacle seems to be winding down. There is a song in what seems to be Chinese. Later, she recognizes the music as Bach. Children part the shadows with flashlights, simulating comets and inspiration, desire and intelligence. The simplicity of this resonates through her with an intensity for which she is absolutely unprepared.

She recognizes that this essential drama is being enacted, in slight variation, throughout the world. White-gowned children sing of the light in remote nations and languages. It is more than a holy day, one holy day or another, but a recognition of the evolution of life. From the fundamental darkness, there is a random juxtaposition of energy, of thought and light. On this night and this night only, Buddha, Christ, Muhammad, and Moses inform the winter waters with a brilliance that glows. Suzanne Cooper finds herself weeping.

When she meets her children after the performance, Mark with his saxophone case, Stephanies still in a white robe, they seem distant and restrained. She notices that they are not carrying their sleeping bags.

"We've decided to go skiing," Mark informs her, barely looking at her.

"That is, if you agree, Mother," Stephanie adds. Her eyes say, Deny me this and I will hate you forever.

Suzanne recognizes that she needs a cigarette. They will go to Aspen and she will go to a 7-Eleven and buy a package of Marlboros. She sees her former husband on the far side of the almost deserted auditorium. Stephanie and Mark are joining their father. They call good-bye to her over their retreating shoulders and this sentiment, at least, sounds authentic. Then she is alone in the auditorium. She walks to the parking lot in the rain, buys a package of cigarettes at a liquor store, and drives to her apartment.

She lies awake smoking and listening to the rain. She has had insomnia since she stopped drinking. She is used to this forced examination of the night while the voice within her demands that she drink. The voice which is male and yet speaks with the cadence of her incarcerated mother, she suddenly realizes.

In the morning Suzanne gets down on her knees and prays to the God she does not believe in to keep her sober one more day. She has been instructed to do this by her sponsor, a woman with eight years of sobriety who has rebuilt her life one painful molecule at a time. Her sponsor did not believe in God in the beginning, either. Suzanne Cooper begins each morning of her sobriety in this fashion, feeling fraudulent and somehow debased. Now it occurs to her that the voice of destruction within her is silent when she prays. She has never noticed this cause-and-effect relationship before.

Something feels as if it is awakening, inside, where she has lived with her secret glaciers, the fields of ice which surround her, which encase her, which keep her protected and inaccessible. The ice which seems pink when the sun chances to touch it. On impulse, she telephones her mother in the hospital. She describes Stephanie in her ankle-length white robe singing about stars in an African dialect. There is something transcendent that she wishes to transmit to her mother. She expects nothing in return, not shared recognition, certainly, not even polite indifference.

"I would have wanted to see this," Candace says from the hospital. Suzanne does not reply. She is looking out her living-room window, into the window of an apartment identical to her own. She can see a Christmas tree and Christmas cards opened across the mantel.

Suddenly Suzanne finds herself offering to pick up her mother. She is telling her mother that she can have a Christmas pass. Suzanne had not planned to see her mother. Candace is too disruptive. It is simply too much pain.

"I'll be good," Candace says, and softer, after a pause, "I promise."

"You won't throw a drink in my face?" Suzanne asks, lighting a cigarette. The package is almost finished. She recognizes that she has started to smoke again.

"I would never do such a thing," Candace replies, voice hurt. "I know you don't drink anymore."

"But I'm smoking," Suzanne reveals.

"You'll stop again, I'm certain," Candace assures her. "You don't drink. That's the important thing."

"The children aren't coming," Suzanne says. She reports the fact of it, simply.

"They will appreciate you when they are older," Candace tells her. "You will see. They will surprise you."

Later, Suzanne Cooper will drive to the hospital, pick up her mother, and carry her suitcase into her apartment near the ocean. Candace will behave appropriately or she will not. They will, perhaps, wear matching white aprons and bake cookies in the form of green stained-glass Christmas trees or they will not. Perhaps they will sit on a bluff above the slow lingering white sails of boats on the Santa Monica Bay, sipping hot chocolate and recalling anecdotes from her childhood. Perhaps Stephanie and Mark will telephone from a ski lodge, suddenly missing her. They might say that Jake and his girlfriend keep the door of their room locked and it doesn't seem like Christmas, really, in that distant lodge, without her.

Of course she will always be disappointed by the traditional demarcations. She accepts this dispassionately. The voices she has internalized will always degrade her efforts and pronounce her inadequate and flawed in all circumstances. They will evaluate the stimuli and tell her she is not loved enough.

But it is this particular morning, following the *Fiesta de las Luces* that occupies her attention. She is hanging up the telephone, staring out the window and taking the morning into her. She is smoking a cigarette in the living room of her apartment in Santa Monica. The storms have stopped. The morning is brilliant with the kind of purified light often seen in high altitudes, a light which implies the revelatory, absolution and forgiveness. It is the light of Christmas and Hanukkah, Ramadan and Kwanza. It is the light of candles on mantels and candles in boats on rivers and moored in harbors in the ports of all the world. It is the light of a billion schoolchildren wearing white robes and white gowns rushing across auditoriums to announce the birth of a myriad of deities. It is the light of children everywhere holding flashlights as they sing into the darkness, and beyond that darkness are great ridges of white mountains covered with white snow and punctuated by uncountable pines, all the massacred trees of Christmas somehow risen and returned. And further, there are green rivers lit by the white of flames in boats. There are ports where rivers empty their caravans of temporary light. And somewhere, in the place above that men perpetually pray to, comets startle the void and inexplicable juxtapositions inspire the darkness into forms of birth.

Suzanne Cooper is smoking a cigarette, racks of cookies

are cooling. Her kitchen curtains are wide open. Sunlight is pouring into the room, brushing against the white apron she is wearing. And she is startled by the thought that she is somehow a candle in the window and she is lit, at this moment, from within.

Naming
Names

WHEN I THINK OF MY ADOLESCENCE, IT IS always afternoon, as if these late-childhood and early-teenage years occurred in a stasis of sunlight filtered through venetian blinds. The light is sliced by strips of gray metal and there is the sense that the boulevard is near. It is inordinately straight and wide and flat, without deviations. It is an artifact of the fifties, when they thought in terms of a central vision, a vast linearity that has since vanished. In my youth, these concepts were still somehow viable. They were part of a code which neither I nor anyone I knew could master. We were aware of the basic principles and how we failed to meet them. We were defiant as a defense. In truth, we lacked the tools necessary for conformity. And we were ashamed.

It is an unremarkable climate I remember as merely warm. The boulevard where I lived was lined with low two-story stucco apartments that had proliferated after the Second World War. These structures were designed to appear innocuous. Perhaps the architects conceived of these dwellings as only temporary. It was a time when living in an apartment was an admission of a defect of character. And it seemed to me then that after the one long boulevard of apartment complexes, there were only residential streets of tract houses for miles in all directions, perhaps to the state line, wherever and whatever that might be.

I would pass these tract houses on my way to Palms Elementary School. The streets were quiet and narrow and lined with trees. Pastel houses were set behind white wooden fences. Intact families lived in such houses. Their mothers stayed home. At Palms Elementary School, the children asked one another whether they lived in houses or apartments. Children who admitted they lived in apartments were consigned to the periphery.

We who lived in these apartments learned that we were unwholesome, somehow cut out of life as it is ordinarily known. We even looked different. Our mothers took the early-morning buses to their jobs. No one braided our hair before school, or put in bows or ironed our collars. No one cooked us breakfast. We were given change. We bought donuts in a coffee shop and ate them as we walked. We crossed the boulevard in heavy traffic, had interactions with adults, and knew about money. We wore our house keys on strings around our necks. We were not like the children in the houses. We didn't have music or ballet lessons after school. And we were always hungry.

In the apartment complex where I lived, the distinctions were subtle. It was necessary to check the apartment number on the door before climbing the fantastically hard cement steps and turning the doorknob. One might have walked down a seemingly identical courtyard path by mistake. It might be 2J and not 4C, after all.

The long courtyard sidewalks were straight and clean. The quiet is dense. It is an era before rock and roll, vandals, graffiti, and litter. The boulevard is a presence, but not yet irrefutably brutal and dangerous. There are no random shootings from cars or gang wars yet, no serial killers who specialize in mutilating girls and women. Drugs are not yet commonplace. They haven't emptied the mental hospitals yet. Torture is unheard of. There is still a notion that we are a civilized country. People are satisfied with an occasional predictable murder by gun.

There is little vegetation along the sidewalks and courtyards and beside the paths along the alley. It is a time before the discovery of potted plants. Urban people do not yet garden. They act as if they are repelled by the earth. There are a few stranded palms near the boulevard, of course, and they are tall and lack distinction. They are some kind of afterthought. Beside the alley, there are trees I did not learn the names of and have never noticed in any other area. These trees produced a plastic-like dark green leaf that felt abrasive to the fingers and did nothing, neither bloom nor fall. There are stray rubber trees near the laundry rooms and slats of a few hardy succulents, but there is nothing vivid or tropical.

This is Los Angeles as it was before the tawdry episodes coalesced into a garish personality. This is how she was before the cosmetic experiments and shabby adventures, when she was ordinary and soft-spoken and dull. She hadn't yet learned to disorient with color, to insist and flaunt and glare. When I looked up at the sky, it was empty. Planes were a rarity. There were still borders. And the sky was large and blue and solid as it should be in childhood.

There were more apartments than you might imagine if you chanced to see these complexes as you drove down Sepulveda Boulevard. The apartments were surprisingly

dense in their width, row upon row. They crowded together, shoulder pressed to shoulder, as if anticipating a
future where one would always be standing in line, at the
unemployment office, at welfare, medicare, and the clinics.
The color of these apartments is prophetic. They are a dirty
tan and the pale green of indifferent foliage beaten by pollution.

You would notice the strident angularity of this world if
you were a child. You would recognize this stretch of Sepulveda Boulevard as being the longest set of blocks you
had ever seen. If you were a child and you chanced to enter
the complex and wind down the center courtyard path, you
would gradually realize that the distance between the boulevard and the alley where the garages and laundry rooms
were was monumental.

It is to this apartment complex on Sepulveda Boulevard
in West Los Angeles that I came with my family to live when
I was nine. We would stay there until I was fourteen. And
there were certain textures and ways in which the sun was
mutilated and the silence magnified that have settled within
me in what I have only recently come to recognize as definitive. We will move when I am a freshman in high school.
By then it was too late.

It is in this apartment complex that I learned to hunt for
and nourish that which was dark, alien, painful, and dangerous. It was here that I developed a capacity to tolerate certain deformations and intrusions that have long
haunted me and are, I suspect, permanent.

I return to this apartment now, in memory, and I am
overwhelmed by a sensation I translate as being unclean.
And I do not physically return, ever. I do not walk down
the winding courtyard sidewalk to the alley and the adjoin-
ing pathways that lead to identical courtyards and apart-

ments. There is no reason to go back. I remember everything.

Every four apartments had a miniature lobby with metal mailboxes divided into four equal slots. There was a kind of wooden trough drilled into the concrete next to it. Now, no doubt, there are Korean and Spanish newspapers. Then, there was only *LIFE*. The ceiling in the small lobby was high. The structure was always dark. The gray cement steps were remarkably cold and hard and no matter how softly I walked, there was a terrible echo.

Noise was forbidden. If you made noise, they could ask you to move. Moving was unthinkable. It would require a first- and last-month rent deposit, a moving truck, new keys. They permitted us to be children, but we were admonished to live through this set of circumstances as quickly as possible and in silence.

The apartment complex was quiet as a cemetery. One never knew who was going to an operation or a treatment, or when. After you went bankrupt, after your insurance ran out and the charity, you were cut when the surgeon could fit you into his schedule. We lived as if we were in combat. And perhaps we were. We awoke and slept at odd intervals. There was the matter of the medications, the pain pills and injections. Sleep was a miraculous state, like grace, and to be guarded. My childhood afternoons were punctuated by the fear of the noise of my school shoes on the steps and the sense that I would be punished for this.

When I think of the years I lived in this apartment complex, I am filled with a sense of secrets, of a landscape soiled and hazardous. The apartments were without obvious character. You couldn't see the death from the outside. I am certain there wasn't even one stray pot of red geraniums to clutter a single walkway. I knew each sidewalk with a singular intimacy. I am a schoolchild, condemned twice a day,

morning and afternoon, to the sidewalk, to a region of asphalt with its dominion of insignificant palms and dull paths
that meant nothing.

Lana Colby lives two apartments in, closer to the alley.
We are in the sixth grade together. She has five brothers,
all of them older. Her father is an alcoholic. It is the first
time I have ever heard this word. It explodes in the room.
It is powerful, a kind of bomb. This alcoholic has deserted
his family. Now Lana's mother must work as a cocktail waitress. And they are Catholics.

Lana Colby is my best friend. She is tall, thin, blond,
and green-eyed. Her sophistication leaves me breathless.
She has her own transistor radio. She is allowed to take
buses by herself. She has a pocket mirror and lipstick. She
can come home when she wants.

My mother disapproves of her. Everything about Lana
Colby is tainted. My parents say she has too many brothers.
This is a startling concept for me, an only child, that there
is such a thing as an abundance of siblings. The way my
mother talks about this implies that having children is somehow volitional. I cannot grasp these implications.

There is something horrible about her father, this man
who drinks too much. I can't imagine how drinking can be
detrimental. He is supposed to take his children out to dinner on Saturday nights and he doesn't come or falls out of
the car. Once I witness this. The car is parked in the alley.
I see the door open and Mr. Colby falls from his seat to
the pavement. I know what to do. I turn away and keep
going.

My parents think it is contemptible that Lana Colby is a
practicing Catholic. We no longer believe in saints. We no
longer worship idols, pray on our knees to bits of stone and
light candles. I am intrigued. I know the world is immeas-
urable in its capacity for betrayal, for evil and cruelty. I

know it is all precarious, all a form of darkness. Of course one must carry mysterious illuminations and speak the names of the powers incessantly.

I go to Dwight D. Eisenhower Junior High now. I walk along the hell of sidewalk twice a day, nineteen blocks, and with each step I say a number. Each number is dedicated to a deity I invent and forget. I engrave the number with my lips and offer it up to a god, a spirit, a demon, and I say, Please, let me live. I envy the symbols Lana Marie wears around her neck, bronze faces she lets me try on. She believes in gods with definite names and attributes. I am amazed.

My mother is talking about the unforgivable crime of Lana Colby's name. Her mother, as if proving her ignorance, has named her daughter for a film star. This is a breach of taste so fundamental, with so many virulent implications, that no explanation seems adequate. It is possible to name a child for a figure from history or mythology or even the Bible, but not from popular culture. Lana is an abomination for which there can be no redemption.

My mother continues to deride Lana Colby's mother, the cocktail waitress. She works at night. My mother returns to this fact as to a perverse fascination. How can any woman work at night? My mother repeats this question every day. Her voice contains outrage and bitterness. I look away from my mother. I am thinking that at least Lana has gods with names and qualities and methods to beseech them. And Lana Colby is more my sister than they will ever know.

Then Roxanne Cohen moves across the courtyard. She has curly red hair and eyeglasses with pink frames. I am racked with jealousy. My eyeglasses come from the clinic. Their shape never alters, year upon year. They are thick plastic and black.

Roxanne Cohen has an eyeglass case with a needlepoint

red rose stitched on it. She has a locket shaped like a heart. But she is still one of us. Her father is in a wheelchair. He has bone cancer. He is turning into powder. And her mother works.

All the mothers in our apartment complex work. The men stay home. This is a world before ambiguity and inversion. This is when there were standard divisions that seemed unassailable and permanent. There were behaviors and attitudes that were like a moral Rocky Mountains, enormous and granite and obviously going to last until the sun blew up. This is when the children at Palms Elementary School asked each other if their mothers worked or stayed home. If your mother worked and you lived in an apartment, your shame and inadequacy were indisputable.

My mother worked. So did Lana Colby's and Roxanne Cohen's. Our fathers stayed home because they were invalids. They had cancer or heart disease or cirrhosis. They were in the midst of surgeries and treatments. Or there were no fathers. They had died or abandoned the family. Sometimes the mothers in our apartment complex were divorced. This was a world where there were still obscenities. The word "divorce" was one of them.

We were allowed to baby-sit for the divorced women. They were the only category lower than us. We felt morally superior. We had no choice in our outcast status. The sickness simply happened. But these divorced women are disgraced. They are without men and we feel they somehow chose this, they brought it on themselves.

When I am twelve I baby-sit for Mrs. Haven. I don't know why she is allowed to call herself Mrs. when she is divorced. Her name is Ivy. I would arrive early with the schoolbooks I did not even make a pretense of opening. Ivy Haven would be getting dressed. She is standing in front of her bathroom mirror. I watch her comb out the pink curlers from her hair, watch her powder and rouge her face, put on lipstick and perfume. Men take her dancing. She is wearing dresses bluer than I thought possible. She lets me feel the skirts. They are taffeta and satin. Even her shoes are blue.

It has never occurred to me that dancing is a possible human behavior, that there are forms for this, procedures, places where this activity is sanctioned. Ivy Haven listens to the radio while she puts on mascara. She drinks wine from a real wineglass. She throws back her head, bounces her auburn curls from side to side, and laughs.

I am stunned. I cannot remember seeing a woman laugh. My mother and the mothers of the children I know come home from their days as clerks and secretaries and receptionists beaten and exhausted. The telephone receiver turns their ears red. Their hands shake. They walk into their apartments prepared for catastrophe, a hemorrhage or a seizure. They know what each dinner will be for the next month. It will be the same. Potatoes, rice, white bread with margarine, hamburger twice a week, oranges, maybe, and in summer, watermelon. We don't have coffee at home. It is too expensive. We drink tap water with sugar in it. Our plates and glasses don't match. We save jars from jam and drink out of them.

Ivy Haven drinks from a real wineglass. She has her fingernails painted in a beauty shop. She can do this because she is going to be on television. She is going to be an actress. She turns her radio on and it is loud. She sings the words of the songs. In her drawers she has pink slips and pink panties folded between scented tissues. Wherever she walks, she leaves a trail of what smells like flowers. There is only silence and death in the apartment where I live. No one turns on the radio. It sits there in case my father wants to listen to a baseball game. It is tuned to the baseball station. I would never dare change it. My parents think that music and perfume and laughter are inappropriate in a world when you know God on a personal level and He abhors you. You open the door of your apartment or look in the mirror and see the proof.

Ivy Haven tells us she is going to be on TV. This is all we talk about, in the laundry rooms and in the lobbies. I even tell my classmates about this. I raise my hand and share this information. Everyone looks at me. I am used to being invisible. I do not have a dog or a cat, fish or turtles, camping trips, grandparents who have a farm. Now I have something to say. I tell them about Ivy Haven. That day, I do not have to eat my lunch on the bench alone.

It is a western. The women wear long dresses with bustles and huge hats with veils. Even my parents watch the program. My father sits up with a blanket wrapped around his shoulders. But Ivy Haven doesn't appear. Later, she explains where she was, sitting in the stagecoach, next to the woman who got to talk and scream at Indians. But no one is interested in this. Because of Ivy Haven I am subjected to ridicule. My parents look at me with disgust. My naïveté angers them. They think I am stupid. They know that no one from our apartments will ever be on television. There will be no redemption, no miracle, no inspired invention.

I am twelve years old and I am in Roxanne Cohen's living room. I know it is dangerous to be in a shared room. There is something terribly wrong with these fathers. They have scars and tubes. They are misshapen, bandaged, broken. Their vocal cords have been removed. Their bones are collapsing. They can't walk, can't breathe, can't wash themselves. And the mothers are gone. We have learned to stay outdoors as much as we can. We play quietly in the lobbies and the laundry rooms alongside the alley. Sometimes a garage is left open and we go inside. We play jacks and Barbies on the garage floor. But today it is too cold. It must be winter. It is raining. That is why I am inside Roxanne Cohen's apartment, in her living room. The venetian blinds slice the air, which is severe and gray. The lamps are on.

Mr. Cohen wheels himself into the room in his wheelchair. I know his name is Mel. Usually, he sits in his bedroom with the light turned off and a newspaper draped across his lap like a blanket. He sits in the shadows that consume the room and pretends to read. Now he is near me. There is something small and sharp about him, birdlike, predatory. I tower over him. He is dark and angry, an offended dwarf with a metal body. He looks unbelievably pale.

"You think I'm an old man," he says, breathless, panting. He wants to talk to me, I understand this. His intensity is terrifying. He is trying desperately to tell me something that I do not want to know.

"You think I'm an old man," he persists, agitated. His teeth are yellow, they look pointed and sharp. Mr. Cohen is grabbing my wrist and pressing it with his fingers. "Look at me," he demands. He is squeezing my wrist. He is hurting me.

I look at him. There is something wrong with his skin. There are red blotches or bruises. The skin looks like it is turning on itself. All our fathers stay home. They bleed. They have emergencies that require paramedics and ambulances. They go into convulsions. You find them on the floor. They turn blue. There are the side effects from the treatments. There is always something.

"I'm thirty-four," Mr. Cohen tells me. "Do you think that's old? Look at me."

I think thirty-four is ancient. I feel nothing. I look at him. I could look at him for centuries and feel nothing. Mr. Cohen begins to cry.

I am running out of Roxanne's apartment. I am angry.

There is a code and Mr. Cohen has broken it. Our mothers cry when they walk home from the buses. We expect this. It seems natural. All mothers cry at night, especially at the end of the month when the money is gone and they are hungry. But the fathers are not supposed to cry. This is unacceptable. They are supposed to be quiet about their malignancies, their recurrences, the radiation treatments that make them vomit, make their hair fall out, their teeth. If they don't behave, the doctors will stop treating them. In between, they need special food like babies. You have to grind it up for them. Sometimes they need ice cream. You drink tap water so you can afford to buy it. Then they forget how to go to the bathroom. This is why you don't want to be alone in these apartments. It is better to wait in the laundry rooms by the alley until the mothers get back. At least their grief is comprehensible.

We learn to smoke cigarettes in the laundry rooms. We sit on the machines and practice drinking. We learn other things from the teenagers. The rooms are deserted. The mothers are too tired to wash on weekdays. Lana has five older brothers. They let us finish their cigarettes and beer. Ernie Colby brings a bottle of vodka down to the laundry room on my thirteenth birthday. He brings a bottle of orange juice and demonstrates how to make a screwdriver. That day, I realize that as long as I can make screwdrivers, I will be able to get through this grotesquerie, this interminable childhood and adolescence.

Roxanne Cohen's father dies. No one is surprised. We know about diseases, know the survival percentages, the prognosis, the evolution of treatment procedures. Bone cancer is incurable. My concept of the world is reaffirmed. He is dead and I am no longer angry.

Christine White moves into the Cohen apartment. The White family has come from Fresno. Christine's brother has leukemia. Her father used to own a gas station. But he had to sell it. Now he works in a gas station. And they had to sell their car. They have come to Los Angeles because of Children's Hospital. There is some vague talk of the City of Hope. I know what the City of Hope is. It is the hospital you never walk out of.

Christine is two years older. But she seems much younger. On the weekends, she bakes cookies with her mother. She wears an apron with a floral print. It's just a question of time before her mother becomes too tired for baking. But now I watch her with almost uncontrollable envy. Christine White has family. This means that there is someone else in the world who cares about her, about them. She has a tangible reality beyond the apartment complex. She has a grandfather who comes and picks her up. She gets taken to Sunday dinner at her aunt's house. She gets Thanksgiving.

Lana and I are enraged. We imagine her Thanksgiving with turkey and mashed potatoes and bowls and platters with flowers painted on them. And chocolates, perhaps, and Coca-Cola. We don't get Thanksgiving, Lana and I. There isn't enough money for turkeys and chocolates. And even if there was, our mothers lack the energy for this, the motivation. Who would they invite? Their blood relatives have decided that they are expendable. They are without family. And there is nothing to be grateful about.

My parents dismiss the White family from their consciousness. Leukemia is incurable. Or worse. Perhaps they will find a treatment and Christine White's brother will linger for a year or even two until he dies. This will force the family to sell the last of their possessions. This will surely send his mother to a mental hospital. That is what happens when one of the incurables has the misfortune of hanging on past their time. The mother can go on for a few months or even a year or a year and a half, walking to the bus, going to her job, taking the bus to the hospital every other night, cleaning the apartment, doing the cooking and the washing, writing the checks for the utilities, sewing seams. A year and a half is standard. After that, the mother breaks down. Then she gets taken to a hospital. Then the fathers start drinking. And the daughters disappear.

I am walking along the kingdom of sidewalk that comprises my version of Los Angeles. The palms are insignificant. I am searching for signs of a mother breaking down. I imagine that one moment the mother is normal, then she stumbles, falls to the ground of Sepulveda Boulevard, broken down like a horse that must be shot. I stand in the indifferent light blue air, a daughter, waiting to disappear. Perhaps today. The sea breeze will take me. I stand at attention on the sidewalk with my eyes closed. I am ready.

The world is divided into the treatables and the incurables. My father has throat cancer. He gets cobalt treatments. He is treatable.

I have already developed my ability to find what is broken and irredeemable. That is why my childhood is informed by these examples of the sick and dying. Perhaps there was something else in this apartment complex, a competing motif. If there was, it spoke in a soft voice and I did not hear it.

Then it is summer. I do not remember the season as an intensity. This is an era of the psyche and body that accommodates the external world and pronounces it tolerable. Summer is a bearable dominion. In the summer, the paths from the alley lead to the sidewalk which connects with a city playground two blocks to the south. I am there every day.

My childhood and adolescence are continuous. I am one day swimming in the city pool of the playground, Palms

Playground, a child with a red rubber bathing cap that cuts uncomfortably at my chin. The next day, I am that same child smoking a cigarette.

It is a warm continuum where nothing ever fits. Not my bathing cap or my bathing suit, my skirts and blouses and one winter sweater. At the clinic, I get a cardboard box of clothing twice a year. This year, the skirt that fit was orange. The sweater I find at the bottom of the box is pink. For six months, my classmates have been mocking me, as though this awful clash of colors had been a deliberate statement of purpose. I feel utterly misunderstood. I am breathless by this indication of the collective stupidity of my classmates. Don't they realize that if I wanted to make a statement, it would be unforgettable?

I am wearing that orange quilted skirt with the pink sweater now. It must be fall. I am buying my first cigarettes in the machine in the laundry room next to the alley. Just beyond the alley, they are building the San Diego Freeway. When I first moved to the apartment complex, there was a harsh brown bean field on the other side of the alley. Then tractors and steamrollers came. It seems as if they've been there for years. They say the highway is going to connect to the north and south, that this is one of the last unfinished pieces. When the highway is whole, it will take you all the way to Mexico.

We don't believe this. Nothing can take us out of this limbo of West Los Angeles. Mexico is an impossible conception, like grace, salvation, and resurrection. It is a word that feels awkward in the mouth, like Paris or Hawaii. These are the words we are not supposed to say. Perhaps the children who live in the pastel houses behind fences can go there, those children who have mothers who stay home, rosebushes, automobiles, and different dinners all the time.

It is said that Mexico is less than two hundred miles away.

It might as well be two billion. The beach at Santa Monica is four miles to the west. It is four hard miles when you are walking in the sun, when you are relentlessly searching for soda bottles that you can trade in for two cents apiece. That will be your lunch and your bus fare back, if it's a good day, if you can find that many. How would it be possible to collect enough pieces of glass to journey to another country?

I am with Lana Colby. The cigarette machine looms enormous in the empty laundry room. It seems to take up the entire wall. We are counting our coins. Lana and I do not know which brand to choose. We buy Pall Mall. We are drawn by the great block of red packaging. We are used to red. We are used to the red implications, the lights of the police cars and sirens and blood. This red is familiar, something we take into our bodies immediately, with intimacy and affection.

Now, in my thirty-ninth year, I sift amongst these ruins of childhood and I can recognize where certain proclivities of my sensibility were formed. For instance, our living room, facing directly onto the sidewalk and boulevard. How sitting on the sofa I would look out the venetian blinds and see a stranger passing a few feet from where I was. How our eyes might meet. The sense of violation near my face. And how I have since refused to inhabit any dwelling without the privacy of a patio, a slat of garden, a hedge. I remember the quality of the darkness in this first apartment, how it was necessary to turn on electric lights even in the California summer afternoons. That is certainly why I have so often managed to live in rooms with terraces and balconies and expanses of glass that drink the sun in.

But those are the details of the surface. I can also locate the intangible psychological residues with precision. There is my concept of the world divided into treatables and incurables. This is a fundamental interpretation which has proved difficult to divest myself of. I can chart the infiltration of this strategy and how I have employed it in relationships and marriages. I think of the ease with which I have discarded identities, professions, circumstances, lovers.

Inevitably, a moment would come where I perceived the configuration, recognizing that it was, at the core, incurable. I could experiment with dosages, change the treatment schedule, so to speak, but why should I? Why let the terminal thing linger? So I took the appropriate action and left it.

I was always able to pack, to walk out, hail a cab and forget. I could say with ease that it had never been. Certainly that apartment in West Los Angeles was where I defined my desire for landscapes devoid of human architectures, for solitude and invention. It was in the apartment complex on Sepulveda Boulevard that I prepared for the inaccessible, the shack on the river near Hana, the farmhouse on the hillside in Majorca.

Just this month, in Kauai, in a condominium in Poipu, an ancient behavior reappeared. I recognized it, but not immediately. I was buying groceries in a town near my vacation rental and I automatically checked a bulletin board for notices of houses and furniture and cars for sale, apartments for rent, jobs offered, baby-sitting and house-cleaning services. I began asking specific questions. Where was the elementary school and the government buildings? How were the streets numbered and what were the winter storms like?

I behaved as if I meant to live in the village of Koloa. I would buy a condominium in Poipu or rent an apartment inland or a shack in the jungle. I could teach English, perhaps, or work as a cocktail waitress at the Westin Hotel in Lihue. I imagined how I would look in my aloha cocktail-waitress uniform, how I would smile into the eyes of Japanese tourists for extra tips. I would wear a double red hibiscus permanently behind my ear. I would take notes for a new novel when the bar was quiet. I could see how the beach would look, ending between mountains with storm clouds, how the ocean might seem Chinese. Perhaps Kauai would not be far enough. There was Borneo and Fiji and they seemed not aberrations but a logical progression into a more delirious green. A green of increasing consequence. A green like a death sentence. The terminal green of no return.

I imagined my daughter in her classroom with Hawaiian children and the children of hotel employees like myself. I wondered if it would be difficult to find a new violin teacher for her and a tutor for French. I was constructing a monthly budget on the side of the envelope containing our return airline tickets when I became aware of the process that had engulfed me. I crossed out the many blue numbers I had contrived. I put the pen down. It was no longer necessary for me to inhabit this particular nightmare of sudden isolation.

Later that day, swimming in a pool in Poipu, in a blue tiled pool built into a cliff above the turquoise bay, I realized that in several days I was going to leave. I was somehow surprised. I remembered that it was not incumbent upon me to remain there; indeed, I had an entire life in another state.

I recognized at that instant, with the sea below a gradation of all possible blues and their resolution, that wherever I have chanced to be across the years, buying gas in Barstow or Las Vegas or changing planes in Philadelphia or Rome, I have always somehow entertained the notion that I was condemned to live there. I have spent agitated and inexplicable hours, elongated noons and pronged nights, gathering survival information. The cost of rentals, what sort of jobs were available, where the hospital and college was. I have been compelled to engage in this behavior relentlessly, year upon year, unaware of the role these thoughts have had in fueling the constant terror that informed my life.

It is only now, as I prepare for my fortieth birthday, that I have freed myself from this obsession. I am no longer compelled to stand weeping on some grim and miserable stretch of windswept highway in the central valley of California or Arizona or Utah, unaware that I was the architect of my unhappiness. Always, I am standing in wind, torturing myself with the expectation that I must somehow begin to live in this miserable truckstop or forsaken town or collection of farmhouses, to strip myself of the details of my former life and embrace this terrible other.

I am convinced that I have spent my life engaged in this perversion of the imagination because of that apartment in West Los Angeles and some child's misinterpretation of events that lodged within, growing as I did, distorting and enlarging inside me. Somehow I recognized that the assortment of treatables and incurables clustered along the courtyard paths and interior sidewalks, these lingering crucifixions, had arrived by accidents of fate and not of their own volition. In my child's version of the world, it must have seemed that if one could be installed in these cages where electric light was necessary even in summer afternoons and strangers walked just steps from your face, if such habitations of chance were ordinary and if one was expected to live there, then one could, without warning, be expected to live anywhere.

It is a cemetery above ground. The mothers are walking

to the buses that take them to their jobs downtown. The treatables and incurables lie in bed bleeding and mute. The mothers return pale, ashen, literally shaken. They are too thin. Food makes them retch. They cry softly. They don't want anyone to see. And they do this every night. It is a time when women who work know they will always work, their bosses will take liberties, if they lose their looks, someone younger will take their job. In between, the neighbors say they are saints. In a year or two, they will break down.

I am in the garage in the alley. I am in the laundry room. I am learning to smoke cigarettes and drink screwdrivers. I am learning attitudes and behaviors it will take me the rest of my life to forget.

I never found out what happened to Roxanne Cohen after her father died. That afternoon is engraved into my nervous system, the thirty-four-year-old man in a wheelchair, how he frightened me on that gray afternoon when rain was falling. Perhaps he didn't want to be merely a passive spectator at his own slow death. Maybe he wanted someone to remember and he sensed that I would and I have.

I don't know what became of Christine White or her brother. They moved back to Fresno seemingly during a weekend when I was otherwise occupied. Childhood is like that. One day they are simply gone. Perhaps I am busy with cigarettes. I am smoking more than a pack a day now. I always have them with me. I find an open garage to crouch in. I have my friends, glowing, red, intrinsic to my private scenery. They help me navigate the treacherous darkness of all things. They are like candles or visual incantations. They placate the void which is mined and has teeth.

It does not occur to me that I could find Christine White's new address and write to her. She is gone and it is as if she had never been. And my heart is hard. After all, she had family, a grandfather who picked her up, an aunt who let her sit at a table with the others for dinner. Maybe she was lucky and that aunt took her in, taught her the intricacies of making stews and soups, asked about her homework, let her try on clothing in front of a mirror in a store. Christine White did not pick up her wardrobe twice a year at the clinic like I did. A cardboard box with your age marked on the side. And if you were too tall or heavy, well, you accommodate.

My father enters into remission. We are moving to a house. I am not excited. Nothing seems to matter. I see Ivy Haven once more. She is also moving. Her settlement has run out. She is moving east, into Hollywood, where it is cheaper, where there are foreigners and robberies and the air is dirty. Hollywood is a sort of incurable condition. It is a form of internal exile, a banishment. One might linger for a while, but the geographic taint and what it implies is permanent.

I am watching Ivy Haven pack. She is placing the slips and pink panties between tissue paper. She is placing these in cardboard boxes. Ivy Haven has failed me for the second time. She wasn't on television like she said she was. Now she was being forced to move. I am watching her packing her clothing. I am thinking that the floral scent, the wine in long-stemmed glasses, and knowing the words and singing along with the music cannot protect you. Ivy Haven seems distracted, sad, or preoccupied. She pretends she doesn't recognize how definitive this eastward move is. She says she will telephone me soon. But she never does.

I keep in sporadic contact with Lana Colby for years. We go to different high schools. I hear she is pregnant. She leaves school. Someone says she gave her baby away.

I am living in Berkeley. I understand that the world is cleanly divided into women who get pregnant and women who don't. I am a feminist. Pregnancy is a tyranny. It is worse than moving to Hollywood. It is incurable and it takes a lifetime to die.

It is several years after college when I chance to run into Lana Colby at the airport. Her mother has died of lung cancer. Her father died in an alcohol ward. Ernie, her oldest brother, the one who bestowed the secret of screwdrivers on me, was killed in Vietman.

Lana Colby imparted this information to me casually, as if she couldn't care less, as if these events had taken place to people she barely knew. She seemed to be in a hurry. She was smoking a cigarette. So was I. I noticed that she did not quite look at me when she spoke. There was something off center about her. I thought she kept her hand near her mouth because she was embarrassed by her crooked teeth. Her eyes seemed large and cluttered with surprise. It occurred to me, later, that she was on drugs.

We spoke for no more than ten minutes. She worked in real estate. She seemed pleased by this. She was divorced, again, she told me. She was vague.

It was just before noon. We were sitting in the bar. We were both drinking vodka. At least I had discovered Bloody Marys. I did not like the way Lana was dressed. I thought her clothing was too tight, too obvious. She wore enormous imitation gold hoop earrings. She seemed somehow unpleasantly ethnic. Her hair was aggressively tinted. She had imperfect grammar. I could hear my mother leaning over my shoulder, employing her stage whisper, saying she'll turn out a waitress like her mother. She'll go bad, you'll see.

I was on my way to Denver. I was giving a poetry reading there. In my briefcase were copies of my poetry book. I did not offer one to Lana. I did not exchange addresses with her. She sold houses in La Jolla now. I thought I would not see her again. Our destinies had been joined and now they were severed. Perhaps we had been meant to impart some impossible-to-calculate word to one another and we had done so.

I was in my late twenties then. My life was a montage of blues and greens, terraces and plazas and roads in the high desert where the skies were littered by mesas of cloud. I thought I was going somewhere. I did not recognize then that I would subconsciously force myself to pretend that I was going to live in each town I chanced to pass through for the next ten years.

I can tell you these things now because I am no longer compelled to create such atrocities of the sensibility for myself, such barbed-wire fences and cemeteries of the soul. I am no longer afraid to name names. I can tell you about Roxanne Cohen and her father and Christine White and her brother, Ivy Haven and Lana Colby because so much time has passed, the incurables have certainly died. And if they have not, I am sure they have forgotten me and why I would wish to betray them.

OVER

THE HILL

SHE LIVES ON THE SIDE OF A MOUNTAIN above Sunset Boulevard in Beverly Hills. The hill rises in the backyard where Frank has built a gazebo. Small square slabs of stone, like the indented plaques on graves in the cemeteries of Los Angeles, form a path to the gazebo. The stones lead past the wooden fence dense with bougainvillea, past the herb garden with its basil and sage, past the circular cluster of rosebushes and the patch planted with annuals, then the stalks of canna and gladiolas and bird of paradise. And the orchids, of course, surrounding one side of the swimming pool.

Jessica sits in the gazebo in the late afternoon. The school bus has brought her children home. Maria is cooking dinner. Jessica waits for sunset as if it were a punctuation that should mean something. At such moments, the city is astonishing with detail. She can see to the south past the Baldwin Hills and the airport and farther, to some ghastly urban infestation one passes only by car when driving to Newport Beach or La Jolla. A place called City of Commerce or City of Industry or some incorporated slum that advertises legal gambling.

From her white wood-slat bench in the gazebo, Jessica can watch the sunset and then the lights of the city asserting themselves, and later, the constant wash of silver and red and green in the sky which are a sort of avant-grade choreography of planes and helicopters. The lights are tiered, they rise from the land and fall from the sky, as if in mute celebration.

"Think of the wildlife Ryan and Ashley have," Frank says. "That's an advantage."

Jessica considers this acre of hill with its iris and roses and borders of bougainvillea, its orange and lemon trees, its hedges of red-and-yellow hibiscus, its bird of paradise and yellow and red and magenta orchids. The gardener made Ashley an old-fashioned swing with rope and a wooden seat. It hangs from the avocado tree and sails out over the hill, over the square indented stones leading to the white wood gazebo. The graves in the cemetery where her father is buried are like these stones. It seems that the dead do not have markers that rise anymore. In this region, they have outlawed idolatry, even in its remote forms. It is near the millennium. We know nothing here will change. We are not waiting for our dead to rise. Even the cemeteries lie in isolated areas, at the end of freeways one has never before heard of. You leave your dead there and never return. You are not afraid of being haunted. The dead could not find you if they wanted to.

But what of the wildlife Frank always mentions? Jessica sits in the gazebo and thinks of the deer, coyotes, squirrels, raccoons, and rabbits that inhabit this acre of hill. Her son, Ryan, is nine. The gardener built a house for him in a tree, a kind of fort with nailed-together pine boards and old curtains in a permanently open window. Ryan has a BB gun and a slingshot. He shoots at anything that moves across the backyard, even cats and dogs belonging to the neighbors. Is his boyhood being enriched by the wildlife?

"Think of the color," Frank says.

She sits in the gazebo and considers the color. The sky is Kauai blue even in August. In the hills where she lives, in these Beverly Hills, the contours remain vivid and assured. These skies are not tainted by smog and the human residues that slope upward from cities. It might be a region in an elemental state of grace. Or a region where pollution has been completely banished, where there has been some complex accommodation. And the greens seem mysteriously illuminated, as if their essences had been somehow defined and freed.

"It's the green of money," Frank says. He is serious.

And the greens contain a kind of crispness, a moist clarity. This is a green you cannot intrude on. It is an absolute assertion. This is the climate that only money can buy. There is no vegetation too exotic or difficult. Here the Japanese and Mexican gardeners arrive at sunrise with bulbs from Australia, China, India, Madagascar, Kauai, and Peru. There should be lilies in the pools, she thinks, and peacocks and jaguars in the tall night grass. Or perhaps they already have this, closer to Sunset Boulevard, in the gated villas she drives past. Or perhaps near the top of Mulholland, where the Persians build their fortresses.

"You have no idea what things cost," Frank points out.

He gives her a computer printout that his accountant has devised. Lists of numbers for services, car insurance, health insurance, homeowners' insurance, gas and water and electricity, food, liquor, chauffeur, car payments, house repairs, school tuition, psychiatrist, swimming pool maintenance, tennis lessons, violin lessons, restaurants, airline and theater tickets, hairdresser, clothing, pediatrician, dentist, orthodontist. There are more numbers, three full pages of them, but Jessica has seen enough.

These numbers are not real, she knows this. Frank's accountant can make numbers appear or disappear. He's not a bookkeeper, Frank likes to say, he's a magician. Now you see it, now you don't. Her husband's accountant creates pages of numbers to substantiate Frank's transitory versions of reality. This is the way Frank's cities are peopled. These are the bridges, the aqueducts and clouds. These are the rituals where one bows to carved stones. These are the slow syllables released into darkness. These are the litanies, the way to bury and raise the dead. These are the creation myths and the cycles of destruction.

"You'll have to economize," Frank tells her. Then he says he won't pay for Westford Academy anymore, or Ashley's violin lessons or Ryan's karate classes. Her children will have to attend public schools. Frank's accountant will make the stocks and bonds disappear. He will make Frank's assets confused and ambiguous. Frank is an attorney. He knows how to go to court, what a judge and jury will find credible. Frank specializes in these matters, these unique parameters. And she will have to rent an apartment in an inferior part of the city where her neighbors will speak languages she does not want to know.

Sometimes Frank takes her to these apartments. They hire real-estate agents for this, usually women who look unhappy. These real-estate agents open the doors of apartments for them. They inspect these town houses and condominiums. They open closest and cabinets. They pull blinds and look where the view should be, but there is none. There is only an alley, a parking lot, or the terrace of the apartment across the courtyard. Always there is a carport with graffiti. And on the terrace, old boxes of diapers and shopping carts upended, a mattress with springs showing, parts of a bicycle, a container for plants, objects that are deprived of context and gutted. Why are these stained things on display? The real-estate agents, who seem to be women just awoken from terrible dreams, women with a fresh sense of small atrocities, offer nothing by way of explanation.

Sometimes Jessica and Frank take the keys. Then they go to these apartments and town houses and condominiums by themselves. They stand on brown carpet that smells somehow of insect repellent and sand, marginal educations and savage divorces, and some anonymous misery that might be random or cyclic or some unearthly confluence of both. They walk across the tiny rooms. She would take only the children's beds and one sofa. There isn't space for more. She begins to feel feverish, breathless and trembling all at once. She thinks this is what malaria must be. We have a kind of emotional malaria now, all of us, poised near the millennium.

"Lie down," Frank says.

She stares at him. They are alone in the town house with the new brown carpet that already looks faded and dull, as if indicative of the sort of dreams one would have here, something inconsequential, intrinsically small, flawed, incapable of transcending itself. She is still staring at Frank, wondering if he realizes she is sick. Is this why he wants her to lie down? And where can she do this, these miniature rooms are empty.

"On the floor," Frank says. "Now."

She lies down on the floor. The ceiling seems to be composed of an immensity of tiny rocks like the surface of the moon. She thinks of the boulevard below, with its decades of balconies where women with their received secrets and tainted memories stand by windows in rain. Or sleep at last with a sense of the moon and the jungle and some ineluctable other. She closes her eyes.

"No. On your hands and knees," Frank says. He sounds annoyed. He has taken off his jacket. He is unbuttoning his shirt.

Later, in the bath, Jessica notices her elbows have been scraped. They are raw. The skin on her knees is red. She knows this injury is called a rug burn. This is not the first time this has happened.

"I don't think you could live in a place like that," Frank says at dinner. "Or could you?"

"No," she quickly agrees. "Of course not."

The maid, Maria, cleans the plates from the table. Ashley is playing a video game upstairs with her best friend, Tiffany. Ryan is spending the night with a friend on a yacht at the Marina. Frank has lit the fire in the den. She can smell wood burning. Frank tells Maria that they will have their brandy by the fire. She hears these instructions occurring across a confused and agitated distance that is inaccessible. She feels as if she is somehow under anesthesia.

Jessica sits on the brick ledge in front of the fireplace. Her body is a series of burns. There is the heat of the fire on her face, the burn of her scraped elbows and knees, and now the cognac in her chest and how she can feel the liquid in her legs and arms.

Outside, in the courtyard between the study windows and the side garden of roses and yellow canna, she can hear the rain fall. Soon it will be time to prepare for the holidays. There will be the shopping, of course, the baking, the wrapping, the decorating of the house and tree and grounds.

There will be the matter of the menus, the wreaths, the Christmas linens and china. She will get a noble pine this year. And perhaps along the iron-slatted perimeter of gate she will have the gardener hang silver lights. Last year they were the only house with red-and-green lights. Everyone else on the street used just silver. We are becoming streamlined and closer to the stars, she thinks.

"Can you imagine Christmas in that apartment?" Frank asks. His voice contains wonder and contempt in equal measure.

She glances at Maria. They look into each other's eyes, startled. Maria leaves a silver tray on the mahogany coffee table in front of the sofa where Frank is sitting. There are grapes and strawberries in a crystal bowl. There is a plate with four types of white cheese. There is larger glass plate with chocolates and raspberry cookies.

"Without a fireplace? Or a dining room?" Frank continues. He is arranging a plate with cheese and fruit and cookies. He hands this to her.

The apartments that Frank takes her to only have living rooms. The dining room has disappeared like the markers on graves. We give our dead indented slabs. We know they are not coming out of the ground. And we don't need dining rooms. We eat standing up in the kitchen or on a sofa in front of the television. A dining room implies a world where a family gathers and shares food. There are no families anymore, only women with children. Is that what one learns from the architecture? Is this how rooms speak?

But yes, she can imagine Christmas in the town house with the brown carpet the color of all the subtle crimes of trapped people. It would rain. She would hang a wreath on the living-room door. She would hold Ashley's hand. She would leave the piano behind. These rooms cannot accommodate pianos. This is a world without musical instruments. In this region, people walk with radios on their heads. But she could still play Mozart on the stereo. Or perhaps she will not be able to afford a record player. But she would have a radio. She is certain of this. Ashley has a dozen radios. Ashley has underwater radios and radios inside stuffed raccoons and bears. She is almost positive Frank will allow the children to take their possessions.

They would have to leave behind the toys that wouldn't fit into a small apartment. She would be getting a two-bedroom apartment. Frank has explained this to her. Ashley and Ryan will have the bedrooms. She will sleep in the living room on a bed that opens from the sofa. And there won't be room for Ashley's dollhouses, for Ryan's electric trains, for Ashley's simulated kitchen with three-foot-high mock appliances, and the easel, the synthesizers, the twin stuffed polar bears with eyes that glow in the dark.

There are moments when she thinks she could divest herself of these things effortlessly, as if they had never been, all the opulent and sophisticated clutter. She could become smaller, less encumbered, a size appropriate to her new surroundings. She could become deceptive, like her circumstances. No one would know what she was thinking.

"You couldn't survive in that apartment. Just you and the children," Frank reminds her.

He is going to recite the separate elements that accumulate and by their density become the illusion of a fact. They are an empty weight. And he is going to tell her exactly what she cannot survive. There is the miniature ugliness, the cheap rugs with their aggrieved and ruined scent and all they imply, the windows with their squalid antiviews of terraces lined with offensive debris where exiled women memorize the textures of premature burial. There are the carports with the names of gangs written in spray paint, there is pavement and no gardens. And her children in public schools where they are the minority and larger children who speak Spanish and Korean and Vietnamese would waylay them in these scars of Southern California alleys. And she would have to wake at seven, even when she has had insomnia and not slept at all, that night or the night before. She will have to rise at seven and make their breakfasts and put their lunches into brown paper bags and drive them to the imposing and dangerous public school. Then she would return to the apartment and clean it, sweep and do the laundry, iron and shop, make the beds, fold her blankets into the hall closet, and transform her bed back into a sofa. She would be required to carry wash to and from a shared laundry facility where coins were necessary.

Jessica wonders how women do this and the other labor of stove and floor, of bathroom, toilet, and tile. How do they master the intricacies of so many surfaces? How is it possible to provide such services and also do conventional work, go to offices, remain the appropriate hours? What happens when your children are sick?

When Jessica reaches this particular juncture, when she imagines the feverish Ashley in an unadorned room in a stucco building ripped by the noise from radios and cars and words shouted in alien languages, Jessica reaches for a glass. She finishes the cognac. Frank pours her another.

"Think of summer there," Frank says. He is looking into her face, as if there was something he expected to find on the surface of her skin. "In the Valley? Without a pool? When its eighty-five here it's a hundred and five there."

It was curious how the outlying areas were assaulted by the elements, how the act of a few miles of geography could produce such dramatic results. The Valley lay between them like the Mojave desert, vast and intractable.

It occurs to her that leaving Frank would be the psychological equivalent of crossing Donner Pass. If she could

survive the leaving, the metaphorical mountains, the hard-
ship of winter, the disease and death and cannibalism, if
she could find the faith and intelligence to outwit this, she
would be delivered. She would come to inhabit another
region entirely. At such moments, she envisions the San
Fernando Valley as it once was, with its unmolested acres
of orange groves and grapefruit trees where blue jays dived
blind into hot nectar. Men came there during the war and
never left. They recognized there was no border to this
valley, no rules to this astonished terrain, with its citrus
orchards, its vistas without obstacles. Here the dead could
be deposited at the end of an off-ramp.

"I won't pay for Dr. Rivers," Frank tells her. "You can't
expect me to."

She has been seeing Dr. Rivers three days a week for two
and a half years. Dr. Rivers wants her to leave Frank. He
wants her to take an apartment in the Valley.

"Where in the Valley?" she asks.

"I don't know the Valley," Dr. Rivers says. He seems
pleased with himself. "I've never been there."

"You've never been there?" she repeats, stunned. Until
Frank began taking her to inspect condominiums, she had
rarely been to the Valley. Or over the hill. That's how the
real-estate agents describe it. Over the hill.

"I'm from western Ohio," Dr. Rivers says.

"But you've lived here for years," she recognizes.
His attitude feeds her fear. She realizes that she hates
him.

"I live on the Westside. My practice is on the Westside.
My patients live on the Westside." Dr. Rivers smiles. It is
simple for him, where and how people live.

"When I move out, Frank won't pay for my treatment,"
she tells Dr. Rivers later that week.

"I think he'll pay," Dr. Rivers says. He is looking out the

window. The window faces the Hollywood Hills. On the other side of the hills is the Valley.

Jessica stares at her psychiatrist. He is absolutely wrong.

"What if Frank refuses?" she continues. "I won't be able to afford coming here."

"Then you can't afford it," Dr. Rivers says. He has picked up a pen. He taps it on the surface of the desk, as if playing an invisible drum.

When she walks into the wind after the session, when she looks at the cold gray slate of autumn sky, it seems possible that she could divest herself of Dr. Rivers effortlessly. She could leave him behind with the piano, the toy dollhouses, the miniature kitchen set with plastic stove and refrigerator, the Ping Pong table, the indoor volleyball equipment, and all that takes up space and gives her nothing.

Now rain is falling. Soon it will be the holidays. She will buy a noble pine as she does every year. She will make Aunt Glenda's St. Louis brownies. She will buy her presents at Neiman-Marcus. Frank's secretary will provide her with a list of names and addresses and a budget. Later, Frank will ask her where she wants to go for her birthday. Her birthday is in January. He will recite the names of cities and resorts, Paris and London, Palm Springs and Hawaii. And she will say Kauai, as she does every year. We have swallows inside us, Jessica thinks suddenly. Our ideas are like walled missions. We return to them again and again, even when they feed us poison.

"Did I hurt you today?" Frank asks. "In the apartment?" He seems somehow hopeful.

Now, because she wants to deny and wound him, she shakes her head no.

"Let me see," Frank says. He is walking toward the fireplace where she sits on the brick ledge with her many concealed flames. He is reaching across the invisible Mojave

Desert that stretches between them, wherever they are. He
is touching her elbow with his lips.

"I have new movies," Frank whispers against her burned
skin.

Jessica saw the bag in a corner of the den, the flagrantly
yellow plastic bag from the video rental shop. Frank thinks
she should enjoy these pornographic movies. He believes
she would enjoy them if she simply let herself. He thinks
she deliberately refuses to allow these images to bring her
pleasure. He does not understand there is no arrangement
of her personality which would allow her to find a sustaining
impulse in these reels. These movies seem to have been
shot in apartments similar to the ones she has been touring.
She can almost smell the anonymous ruined brown carpeting. Beyond the curtained windows, Jessica thinks, are
streets where we are always cold and know small atrocities
by lamplight. Here the sea is remembered and the propor-
tions of the heart are washed by thoughts of ancient places
and orchids the color of silence. In these apartments young
women are taken with force. There are lurid combinations.
Women with burns on their elbows and knees.

"I saw Monty," Frank is telling her, his voice soft. "He
came by the office."

Monty is Frank's drug connection. What Frank is really
saying is that he has cocaine and pornographic movies. He
thinks this is somehow an inducement for her. Frank is a
divorce lawyer, after all. They have been married sixteen
years. Frank thinks he knows the parameters of acceptable
marital behavior. It's his specialty. He thinks this is how
people live.

She closes her eyes. The rain is falling harder now. The
windowpanes radiate a chill. It is probably only a drizzle in
the Valley, she thinks, or a light mist. She imagines this
mist falling across the wide boulevards with their relentless

rows of condominiums and their alleys of carports brutalized by graffiti, by trash, by stolen and abandoned shopping carts. The Valley is a vast plain stretching indefinitely to the feet of the barren and hallucinatory mountains. In this Valley lie the living graves of women at the millennium. It is a grid of town-house condominiums where women live alone or alone with children. Women who had nervous breakdowns but can no longer afford treatment. Children who leave behind their dollhouses and violin lessons to come to apartments where they do not speak the languages of their neighbors. They watch television in the long afternoons until their mothers return from work. When the children are sick, special arrangements are made. When she solves this equation, when she can understand what they do with the sick children, then she will be able to leave. Perhaps she could ask someone. The woman who does her manicure, perhaps. Or the clerk at the cleaners. Or even her maid. Maybe Maria knows.

She imagines that she is standing on a balcony of an apartment where she lives alone with her children. It is a moment when she knows there is only earth and silence and a trembling in crowds in all the ruined latitudes. And how we wake to sudden clarities and men with knives and mesas and years. How we know that we are simply bodies with hands, words, and blood in nights of impossible gatherings beneath jacaranda trees.

"Your knees?" Frank is repeating. "Are they scraped, too?" He is finished with her arms. He is standing. He is balanced like a baseball catcher in front of the fireplace. He is lifting her robe and studying her knees. He is bringing his face to her legs.

Now there is the rain falling. Now there are her clandestine flames. And how one day she is going to leave. She is certain. She will simply walk out in the morning, as if she were going to the gym or the florist or a medical appointment. She will drive over Mulholland instead, down into the enormous concrete mouth of the Valley. One day she will go over the hill. She will take her children and nothing else and this divestiture will free her. It will be like crossing Donner Pass. It will be the end of isolation and spiritual starvation. It will be what happens after a woman has been alone with prophecies of cancer and water and madness and savage inhabitations in the primitive country. It will be like returning in the last light, in the same transparencies where we long for boats and splendor. It will be like discovering that time and space are indeed a continuum. It will be like arriving in another century. It will be like finding God.

POINTS OF
DECISION

JESSICA MOORE GOES TO KAUAI FOR HER fortieth birthday. It is as if turning forty were the psychological equivalent of a physical phenomenon, a comet perhaps, and she has chosen the most beneficial area in which to observe this spectacular event. There will be gradations in the preceding days, then the eve of the actual dawn, day, and night of it. Then there will be the day after when she will be somehow and permanently different.

First the green pull of Lihue Airport. The small plane from Honolulu seems to barely miss the sudden mountains that rise out of nowhere, flaunting themselves. The mountains are a green without reservation, like a form of enlightenment. Then there is the tentative landing at the miniature airport. The sense that the air itself is extreme, as if electrified or blessed. The air seems charged, altered in a manner that makes her think of drugs or God.

She walks down the metal steps from the plane. You do

not enter Kauai through terminals but touch the ground immediately, walk in and through it, becoming part of the elements. As she touches the asphalt and feels the wind, she realizes that this is a ritual of repetition. At this moment precisely, she always thinks it is impossible that she could have ever left. Certainly there could be no circumstance compelling enough to require that she depart the islands. If it came to it, she could sleep on the beach and beg scraps at the back doors of restaurants. She could wait on the sand like the stray cats. Later, she could find some pot grower in the interior who would have her. They could live in a bamboo and chicken-wire shack without electricity on a river without a name where the borders are anthurium, orchids, and torch ginger. Or she could have sex for money with Japanese and Korean tourists at the Westin. She could do this with a suntan. She would look young enough.

Jessica Moore leans back into the leather of the black limousine. As the green unfolds in front of her, she remembers that this is the only place she has ever been that is better than the postcards. All other cities and ports have been a disappointment, the actuality was less dramatic and intense than the photographs. Always the reality was a clutter, a sense of debris and degradation, exiled history, smog, amputated gods, and misery in the streets, in the alleys and the terraces. Always afternoon became compromised and indifferent. And the museums and taxi drivers were on strike.

The Hawaiian Islands are the exception. It has something to do with the motion, she decides, the way the wind blows the palms and the air becomes aroused. The sky with its clouds in constant transition. The waves relentlessly breaking. The geometries above and below ceaselessly, second upon second, re-forming. Photographs make landscapes seem conventional. The islands defy such linear assumptions. There is nothing simple about them.

"Are you happy?" Frank asks.

They are riding through an unexpected tunnel of eucalyptus bordering the road between Lihue and Poipu. The road seems to vanish into canefields, into a seamless intelligence. The green is literally unspeakable. It would be a violation to reveal this landscape to anyone.

It occurs to her that there are experiences of inexpressible intensity that one immediately forgets. It is too disorienting and painful to remember, like childbirth, of course, and sexual obsession. And the certainty of God in moments of disintegration. There is the furthermost range of intoxication such as LSD and injecting narcotics. And there is Hawaii. There is this green, this jungle with its verdant altitudes and exaggerations.

Beyond the car window, the green reveals itself in a slow striptease, as the density becomes ti plants and pili grass, umbrella and papaya trees, plumeria and ginger. Happy is an insufficient concept. She glances at Frank but finds it impossible to reply.

"You're doing it again," Frank tells her. "Every damn thing I say. I feel like you're grading me, giving me D's."

Jessica wonders why he employs that particular image of the schoolteacher. It's been years since she taught a single class. That was when she had to leave abruptly, before the quarter was over. She was teaching twentieth-century poetry that year. It was when her father died.

Frank is still looking at her. She takes his hand because that is easier. She smiles and touches her lip with one vertical finger and breathes softly against it. The sound is a miniature green shush in the clarified noon, a rustling of ferns perhaps, or the wind in pili grass. It is a small green sound that barely intrudes and slides back into the jungle and is gone.

Later she unpacks in the same room they had last summer. It is the room Frank said she requested. It opens onto a grassy promontory she does not remember. It is early afternoon. She sits on the grass. The ocean is directly in front of her and to her left and right. Exactly half the world that she can see now is water, uninterrupted, a series of blue and purple and turquoise gradations between her face and Australia. It will come from the ocean, she decides. This way she can watch it separate itself from the languid horizon. Space and time coalesce here in the neon waters of Poipu. She plans to watch forty come off the water, tangible, approaching like a sailing ship. It can sail into the cove at her feet. It can anchor between her legs.

There are implications in these blues that she is missing. If she took a line of cocaine, she could understand the assertions in these colors, the direction of their intentions. She could know the peninsula in its nuances, how it smells newborn, with a hint of rain, of plumeria, of virescent moonlight. And in the sky, the clouds weigh nothing.

Jessica finds herself walking back to her hotel room. She locks the bathroom door. She opens her compact, removes the powder, creates a line of it across the tile counter. She breathes it in and her body feels whole again.

Yes, now it is divesting itself of subterfuge. She can look beneath the overwhelming green-and-blue surface. She can decode currents in the water and air. She is wondering if there were only green, would it be a form of truth, the way avenues are and mathematics, airport schedules and doorbells and how we answer? If there were only these assertions of grace and purity, these blues and greens, would we take our names from birds and the curvatures of wind? Would we worship the singular definitions the waves and trade winds bring? And always the sky is young, surprising, without division. It could make love all night. It could bring you mangoes and all the green things you have imagined.

"What are you thinking?" Franks asks. He has walked out on the promontory. He bends down near her, balancing like a catcher. He is exactly as he was, only less. His hair and face have thinned. There is nothing unusual about him anymore. He becomes more generic every year. When she sees him across a hotel lobby or airport terminal, she thinks he could be anybody's husband. They might have assigned him to her based on a statistical interpretation.

She closes her eyes. She decides she will say the first thing that comes into her mind, the first shape, the first shy syllable unfolding like a kind of origami in the void. It's the room with the shells and bones and sea maps, the room of glass overlooking the ocean. It is the place she imagines Isla Negra to be. Isla Negra where Neruda lived. It is the Neruda of his final years, the poet with cancer. She envisions his study as being composed of three sides of window above a dolphin blue ocean. From there, in the long afternoons, he can see his sea skeletons float like kelp on the waves. Later they will be gutted by moon. He sits here, refining his vocabulary of marine things with their fins and liquid destinies, with their eyes locked in moist corridors where their fortunes are exposed in a colossus of salt.

"I was thinking of Neruda, in Isla Negra, with cancer," she reveals.

Frank is staring at her. "You said the same thing on the plane this morning. When I asked what you were thinking."

"Really?" She remembers she had poured herself a glass of wine. She takes a sip. "That's curious."

She would never ask someone what they were thinking. It's a matter of eddies and pathways, each with their own immensity of blue-and-green terrains, entire evolutions, dynasties, orbits. Neruda had his marine passions and hier-archies, his archaic beaches filled with creatures aching for completion beneath currents of arrested possibilities. In the shadows are the frail geometries of love. Perhaps they are waiting for the waves to redeem them. Then they could be deathless, resurrected, infinitely alert in those deceptive female worlds.

Of course, Frank doesn't want to know what images fill her mind. He is simply checking her condition. He takes soundings. As if she would actually say, Darling, I am sifting through the bones of this blue afternoon and preparing to drown myself.

He offers her some red thing, some exiled flame, perhaps. No, a flower. An anthurium or a hibiscus. Yes, a red hibiscus. She takes it and places it behind her ear.

She draws a long line of cocaine across the tile counter before she joins her husband for dinner. She snaps her compact with the drug shut. She stares into her eyes in the mirror. I am forty and tropical, she thinks, torch ginger grows near my mouth. These are the red lamps of the islands, the red lamps of mythology. It is the red of hibiscus, of course. All the deserted women on the balconies and wharves nod their heads in unison. They know this, the women with the one last red rose in their silent mouths. And how the red lingers, like love exhausted by its possibilities and some innate squalor.

"You're not going to talk about death and disease," Frank says softly. They are walking near the swimming pool, with its fountains in the center, shadows forming just below the blue surface, as if something was swimming up from below. They are crossing blue-and-white tiles to the hotel lobby. It occurs to her that Frank is issuing a warning. "You promised, remember?"

She nods. There is no cancer in Isla Negra, she thinks.

Cancer has been banished. There is Neruda sitting in his study. He will live forever. Below, the whales are passing south, swelling the ocean with intelligence. It is a manifestation of the process, the blue divinities only and the palms in the flagrant renegade air. It is the punctuation of red hibiscus and torch ginger near my cheek only. It is the essences of heretics in my hair, that is the fragrance, that and the sound of waves tame after storms.

They sit at a table facing the ocean. It is the beginning of sunset. The sea is the purple of a shell, glazed and translucent. The sky is the interior of an abalone shell, mother-of-pearl. The sunset streaks the sky with glistening peach. The air is rose, a benediction upon the ocean or a new tattoo. The clouds are backlit, a chain of islands above the darkening bay. The world is inverted, mirrored, dreaming landmasses into three dimensions. The evening seems to contain pathways with glittering metallic edges.

"I thought you weren't drinking," Frank says.

"It's only wine," Jessica replies, lightly. "It's nearly my birthday."

"Are you doing cocaine, too?" Frank is staring at her.

"Of course not." She dismisses the thought. There is no cancer in Isla Negra. There is no cocaine.

Frank removes his eyes from her face. The sun is a red fist. Of course, Neruda knew he had cancer. He too watched the sunset, that particular moment just before the precocious moon, the instant when the reefs are uncovered. It is at that juncture that time is absolutely fluid. If you watch the water, you will see everything. Somewhere a god is being born, to gather the wayward waves, the ransacked winds, the skeletons of drowned horses and dolphins, the poppies, the volcanoes, and the throats dense with prayer.

After dinner, they walk to their room along a pathway

built across sand. There are torches on the coconut palms. The torches are the only light on the peninsula. She is listening to the waves. Perhaps they are a kind of narrative. The clouds, the full moon, and the stars that form a lucid confederation. The stars have ancient boundaries. But they are anchored, she recognizes, not fixed.

She takes off her makeup and washes her face. She sniffs more cocaine. Then she lies still on their bed. Frank is looking at her with an expression she cannot interpret. She closes her eyes. She is thinking that the moments of one's life are mute associations informed by our slow comings and goings, our reasons and unpackings beside the shrill lamps. She is thinking if Frank touches her, she is going to scream.

It is better in the morning. She orders champagne with breakfast. It is nearly her fortieth birthday, after all. It's the countdown now. There are only two more days. Then she will have crossed that line and entered into some other she cannot even begin to imagine. Perhaps it will be a splendor, a sudden conflagration of wild philodendron and trumpet vines. Perhaps there will be jungle birds and stones the sea has polished.

She sits on the promontory thinking that she can remain there until it comes, synthesis, the sailing ship peeling itself off the horizon. She will face the singular waters until it comes with its relentless blue hands, with its subtle inks and lies, its sophisticated hieroglyphics.

"You haven't moved all day," Frank says. It's an accusation.

Jessica knows how Frank spent the day. He went scuba diving off Shipwreck Beach in the morning. He took underwater photographs. Then he dived for shells. Later he swam one hundred laps in the hotel pool. This is how he charts his landscape. He must take something from this world, if only a picture or a tiny top shell. He must feel he possesses it, literally. If he swims, he is compelled to count the laps. He must place his concept of precision and quantity on the liquid blue face.

Now he is spreading out a map of the island. This is the context. The possibilities are finite. It is necessary that she enter into this needless set of fraudulent boundaries. No, she doesn't want to take a helicopter to Niihau, the forbidden island. It is forbidden for a reason, no doubt. And she does not want to raft, jeep, kayak, fish, or dive. She doesn't want to take anything from this place.

Jessica selects a drive to Princeville as being the least offensive of her limited possibilities. When Frank goes to make the arrangements, she scoops cocaine with her fingernails and inhales it, quickly, once, twice. She carries the drug with her now, in the beach bag. She can spend the entire day and night on the promontory. She has everything she needs. At night she counts the stars. She can feel the hard pulses of energy on her cheeks. She can feel the silver infiltrating her skin and her conventions.

In the morning, as they are getting into the car, Jessica knows Princeville is a mistake. It is the day before her fortieth birthday. The signs are subtle and bear careful analysis, an augury of tenderest intimacy. It should be a day of slow motion and ritual postures, of noting the liquid wind, the scent of spice at dawn and noon with its green contingencies. Later, there will be the way the sunset seems to flame and smoke and call, obsessively avenge itself.

Because she wants to slow this senseless trip down, the way Frank assaults the landscape, how he grinds it under the wheels, she asks him to stop at the Wailua River in Kapaa. He stops. There are tour boats. They find a seat. The wood smells damp and old and corrupt. Everyone else on the boat is Japanese, a tour group of young couples wearing cameras and leis and whispering. Then they are moving up the Wailua River. It seems to run down from the interior out of nothing, a green without moderation or lighthouses or satellites. It does as it chooses.

At the front of the boat, two Hawaiian men wearing aloha shirts and dirty blue jeans appear. A plump Hawaiian girl joins them and begins an uninspired hula while the men play "Blue Hawaii," the Elvis Presley song, on their guitars. They are going up the river to a fern grotto sacred to the ancient Hawaiian people. Now it can be rented. Japanese marry there. And the Hawaiians are smiling as they sing the Presley song. The Japanese are taking photographs and movies of this. The Japanese have both types of camera. The moment is a borderless obscenity, a perversion of at least three cultures simultaneously, she decides.

Then, suddenly, Jessica begins to wonder what the musicians and dancer are paid. It might be possible for her to find employment as a hula dancer on a tourist boat. She could go up the Wailua River daily, to the fern grotto, while Japanese took her picture and put her into their movies. She imagines herself on display, later, in films shown to neighbors in suburbs of Toyko. She would wear a yellow or red hibiscus, shell earrings. She would be permanently tan. She would be draped in printed fabrics of flowers, orchids and plumeria. She would smell like the jungle.

She would stand at the front of the boat and recite the alphabet of greenery along the bank. She would explain to tourists how the green density was really ti leaves, the plant they made hula skirts from. And the breadfruit trees came from Tahiti. And beside the river were pili grass and bird of paradise, red bananas, Kona coffee trees, umbrella and papaya and nut trees. If they asked, she would enumerate the red elements of the jungle, which were anthurium, torch ginger, orchids, and hibiscus.

Jessica recognizes this fantasy. For years she has been haunted by the feeling that she must jump ship wherever she is and somehow adapt to the local environment, however alien or hostile. Whenever she changed planes, in Oakland or London, stopped for gas in Spokane or Houston, she was tormented by the sense that she must find a place to live there, a job, a situation. She is aware of the fact that her thoughts are virulent and inappropriate. Still, she finds it difficult to stop. She wants to pursue this further, to ask for the details of this life. Does one always have the same boat or does one change according to some rotating schedule? Where do the musicians live? Could she study hula on Kauai? Could she sleep on the boat?

"You're pale," Frank observes. "You look like you're going to throw up. Are you taking pills again?"

"I'm fine." She smiles.

Jessica has learned how to put her hand into her beach bag, find her compact, snap it open, and extract cocaine in her fingernail without looking down. Or she can hold the compact open, as if she were just adjusting her lipstick in the mirror. No one would see the drug she places beneath her nostrils and breathes in. That's what she does now, on the Wailua River.

They stop for lunch in Kapaa. She locks the door of the ladies' room and draws four lines of cocaine, she does these quickly and draws another four. It's a local café. The plastic tablecloth is dirty. The fan is broken. The window is smeared. She thinks she should keep track of how much cocaine she is sniffing. Perhaps she should devise a strategy, invent a border. But this is the eve of her birthday and there are no rules that apply.

After lunch, after she successfully rearranges the food on her plate to give the appearance of having eaten something, after she moves the pineapple and mango slices from one side of the plate to another and back again, they walk through Kapaa. Kapaa is shabby boutiques and stores that sell seashells that have been made into wind chimes and picture frames.

She has noticed the cemetery before, perhaps on other vacations in Kauai. But now she is drawn to study it. The cemetery is in the enclosure of a church near the center of town. Here the dead lie under stone markers, as if their life and death meant something. It isn't like Los Angeles, where the dead get a small plaque indented in the brown grass above their gutted chests. Here ti plants and ginger grow on the dead. Plumeria falls on them and the prehistoric rain and the random inspired things the trade winds bring, like metals for bartering and conch shells from the Philippines; cowrie shells to be strung and used as currency; rumors, whispers and litanies. Here the dead have the constant sense of stars above and dolphins in the water and passages where there are whales. There is a sense that the oceans and skies are inhabited and nothing is mute.

Here death would not be anonymous, Jessica thinks. This ground would know you. You could trust and lean into it. On Sunday, you would see what your children are wearing to Mass. You would remember the purple orchids on that particular blouse, the way pink plumeria are printed along the neck of his skirt like a wreath.

You would know your daughter would pass on her way to market. You would lie next to the church, across from the bakery, the fish store. You could have the same place in death as you did in life, you could be a central fact. And even the most careless of your children would give you flowers and shells and speak your name out loud.

In Los Angeles, they bury you off a freeway that is unfamiliar. You leave your dead there, in some suburb you will never see again, not by plan or accident. No one asks you where your father is. There is barely time for the living.

"Don't say it," Frank cautions.

"What?" She is wearing sunglasses. He can't really see her face.

"You want to be buried here." Frank seems sad and angry simultaneously. She realizes that she can no longer read this man at all. "You do this in every goddamn small town. Christ. You're like clockwork. Don't even say it."

Jessica closes her eyes. She can smell the air laden with what the trade winds have brought, the spices, the engraved continents, the lyrics for songs and calendars with ritual days assigned to various gods. These gods are remembered for specific actions. They marry and father children and commit suicide.

In the car, as they drive back to Lihue and the hotel in Poipu, she begins to cry. She doesn't have to go to Princeville after all. There has been some subtle intercession. Frank unlocks the hotel room and leaves her alone. She puts the powder into her nose. She walks out to the grassy promontory. She looks at the horizon with two ships on it. Just after sunset, there will be six stars.

Frank takes her to Lihue for her birthday dinner. The limousine leaves them in front of the Westin. They ride in a horse-drawn carriage. She is wearing a white dress Frank bought her last year in Mexico. He places a pink plumeria lei on her neck. She has a pink hibiscus pinned behind her left ear. When she closes her eyes, she smells flowers.

The night is hot. They walk past the five interconnecting swimming pools with their strange gazebos and bridges. She notices women serving cocktails near the pool. They wear short pieces of flower-print fabrics as skirts. They have pink hibiscus in their hair. She would look satisfactory in such an outfit, carrying a tray of drinks. Someone at the hotel would get drugs for her. She could live in Lihue.

They are standing between the pool and the beach, as if they are in an uncertain transition. It is sunset. It is the first sunset of her fortieth year. She keeps walking ahead of Frank. Finally, he seems to understand. After a moment Frank sits down on the rocks above the beach. She sits down in a chaise longue on the sand.

She has been thinking about her father today. She thinks these memories are intrusions of clarity. She can remember herself at seven and seventeen. She can remember the day her father committed suicide. It was a Sunday in January. They couldn't find her for three days. She almost missed the funeral.

When the sun sets, she is going to walk back to the rocks where Frank is sitting. She is going to tell him that she wants a divorce. When Frank asks her where she plans to live, she won't be frightened. It won't be like the Sundays when Frank has taken her out with real-estate agents, when they stopped at tract houses on wide gray boulevards with broken screen doors and square lawns of irredeemable urban foliage, brown and half-dead that cost half a million dollars. Frank does this to frighten her. He makes her stand on the terraces of apartments that face onto other terraces filled with children's toys and bedsprings and pieces of rusty appliances. This time when Frank asks where she will go, she will say, "I'll rent an apartment in West Hollywood or the Valley."

Then Frank will say, "What about Ryan and Ashley?"

Ryan is eleven. Ashley is nine. They are with Frank's mother in Los Angeles now. When Frank says, "You'd lose a custody battle," she will shrug. She will say, softly, "Maybe so."

"You can't afford to go to court," Frank will tell her.

Frank is a lawyer. He doesn't think anyone can afford to go to court. Of course, he has colleagues who will serve as his attorneys. It won't cost him anything. Frank has many times named the potential men who will represent him. David. Marty. Jerry. She is supposed to pretend she doesn't know these men are conspiring to take her children away and leave her destitute. She is supposed to behave as if Frank has revealed nothing when she meets these men at the club. She stands there, in a lobby or a bar, feeling as if her life were taking place in another century entirely.

Then Frank will say, "You realize you'll probably never be able to afford the Westin again?"

She will nod her head, yes, yes, she knows and understands. But now she wants to remember this sunset, the first of her fortieth year. She wants to remember how the beach looks. She stares at it now. It looks cold. The quality of the sun has shifted and been diluted. Now the cliffs seem inaccessible, too green and moist for anything to live on them.

She had intimated that she wanted a divorce last year. That is when Frank began taking her to condominiums and apartments, making her open drawers and cabinets and terraces and breathe in the smell of the brown carpeting with its scent of heartbreak and insect repellent and some pervasive anonymous misery that has fallen into the fiber of the rug itself. Last year, she was still somehow vague and open to interpretation. Frank said, "Jesus, I've had it. I'm going to sell the house, go abroad. There's a government program that interests me. It's like the Peace Corps for businessmen. I've already applied."

She had nodded her head then, not in agreement but in an attempt to clear it. The concept of Frank, who became enraged if the car he ordered was the wrong color, going off to share his expertise in a third world country was ludicrous. Frank actually imagined himself donating skills in the Amazon or India. She wondered what his skills were, precisely. Phoning his broker? Conspiring to remove young children from their mothers? Taking photographs of forbidden territories?

Jessica glances at the sky. It's a bearable sunset, not too flamboyant, not the sort that makes you want to reach into your own flesh and tear pieces from it, that's how much the colors hurt. There are no clouds that seem like mountain ranges rising out of the waves, at least not yet.

Perhaps she should feel a spasm of tenderness for this man who has revealed his squalid inner life to her. By extension, she knows the secret lives of women who cannot tolerate water stains on their glasses envisioning themselves in Borneo or Java, ridding swamps of malaria, planting the crop. This is what we do, silently, subconsciously, we are lurching enchanted between the implausible. Men wait for their piña coladas, vowing to become charter-fishing-boat captains if the investigation reaches the proportion of a scandal. Men who cannot read the stars or a city map are planning to navigate a borderless green in hurricane season.

The beach faces two separate pieces of peninsula. Mountains with coconut palms are in front of her. To the left, the land seems a lime afterthought. And between the land there is a thin channel of water, then the ocean. Now the other side of the channel looks delicate and Oriental, smudged and pink.

Frank is standing near her. He leans over, pointing his words at her. "I know," he says. "You want a divorce. You say that every birthday."

She looks at the sunset. It occurs to her that it is way after the apocalypse. It is so far past the apocalypse that the colors are still otherworldly and unnamable, but they no longer promise certain death. They are a danger, yes, but one can outwit it. One can survive this partial extinction. Afterward, one is strangely altered.

The stray pink is rising. It is metastasizing above the cliffs. It is a lavender wash strung with pink. There is a plane midway across the channel. Everything is light.

It is this sense of light infiltrating her that is an astonishment. The light is illuminating her failures, her stasis and impossibilities. Nothing matters but this light. That's what Neruda would think, at sunset, in Isla Negra, with his terminal cancer. The whales are passing to the south. There are the shelves of shells, the dust that comes off bone and all ancient things. There is a moment of light at a particular juncture in the sunset, a light so utterly without knowledge of man, so indifferent to humanity, that it has no category at all. It is not relevant to number this exceptional sunset, she decides, to judge or label it. And it's changing. Can there be some communication between them, some interplay? And the sky like a volcanic eruption, a fierce glowing orange on the top and bottom, and between these flames, a field of absolute purple.

Somewhere the Wailua River with its tawdry musicians and hula dancers is winding down to the ocean. The river is falling asleep, dreaming of sea bells and a violent completion. The river winds past the grotto of mourning where ferns grow out of solid lava rock. Later the wind will turn green and suggestive, indecent. She will want to rend her clothes, here where nothing is vacant, unmated, not even the ocean at night with all its openings, its points of green decision. At sunset, cities always rise from the waves. They suspend their hallucinatory architectures above the water. They perform miracles. Skylines are repeated in triplicate, in labyrinths and fluid mockeries of stone. These are the ruins of the future.

"Come on," Frank says. He's annoyed. "It's getting cold."
He is holding out her shawl for her.

Everywhere men and women sit at bars and restaurant
tables, on chaise longues, at the blue tiled sides of pools
and on beaches. They are going to become pilots and gui-
tarists and cardsharps, nurses and hula dancers and cour-
tesans. The fields of sky above go from purple to a black
like burned wood, beads that are used in prayer and something delicate, like breath and stars and infants. And we
are all slaves of the resurrection, Jessica Moore is thinking,
the currents, the cycles, the small evolutions of the mouth.

Frank is standing between her and the hotel. He is holding her green silk shawl. It lies in the cool air between them
like a kind of banner. It's another portal, another point of
green decision. The planet is webbed with these intricate
pathways. These points fall where they may, in Poipu and
Los Angeles and Isla Negra. Nothing is remote. Somewhere, now, it is day. Somewhere, now, it is a festival for
a god. They are releasing turtles into the river in celebration
in an uncorrupted noon, green as glass, relentless and
wanton as an opium dream. Somewhere it is noon on the
river. Beneath silk banners and dazed palms they are releasing turtles and tossing scorched orchids women in August kissed.

If she were to begin running, that would mean something. If she were to turn from the hotel and start running
along the lip of the ocean, south where the peninsula nar-
rows and disappears and the ocean runs through a channel
of rock and turns Oriental and strange, ancient and pastel,
that would be a statement and an answer. She can see the
green on the land above the water, the sort of green a
woman could know and embrace and say yes.

Frank is pointing his words at her. Then he is gone. That
is what happens when you run at night, the darkness takes

your enemy. It's been so long since she ran, she has forgotten how effortless it is, how you let the wind and water guide you, how stars open above your face. And you take what the trade winds bring, seeds, the principles of aerodynamics, kites and origami, edible plants, shells, the tangible increments of survival. And running is like flying, you must divest yourself of everything but purpose. The beach bag, the drugs, the lipstick, the wallet with your false identities. You don't need this. You never needed it. You need only the lean elements of your body and the knowledge that at last and finally you are running for your life.

DESERT

BLUES

Desert

Blues

EVERYTHING WAS COLD AND BLUE ALL THE time. There were no longer any increments or divisions. Diana Barrington was surprised by how much she missed them, lines and frontiers, clocks and dates and the debris of convention that she had insisted on divesting herself of. Now there was only the icy blue, Baltic blue agony. She felt as if fierce angular waves rose and broke behind her face.

"Why don't we take your psychotic episode across state lines?" Carlotta McKay asked. It was an undifferentiated drained blue afternoon in the flats of Hollywood. The air seemed comprised of failed neon and exiled particles without name. Outside, palms stood in a faded blue stasis like the culmination of centuries of brutal indifference.

It occurred to Diana Barrington that she liked the way her best friend talked about crossing state lines. There was a charge to her words, something in Carlotta's voice contained a specific intonation of the amoral. A blue flash of Rimbaud, perhaps, smuggling contraband.

"We could take your nervous breakdown on vacation," Carlotta McKay was saying. She was staring at her. "Give your nervous breakdown a break. What do you say?"

Diana Barrington formed a miniature blue "okay" with her lips but her mouth remained sealed shut. Speech was an evolutionary development that had not yet been perfected for her, lips and tongue in predictable cooperation, reliable vocal cords. Diana tried again. She listened for a sound and there was none. Somewhere, blue fins dipped into bands of aquamarine water, a lagoon just past sunset where the tropics wind down, breathless after dynasties of orchids, hurricanes, and syphilis. Somewhere, something ambiguous began to swim.

Okay, Diana Barrington thought, okay, let's do it. She wanted to say this but she lacked the capacity to push the sounds out. They were like stones offshore, constantly engraved by waves and the blue motion. There are only these blue repetitions, after all, Diana realized. Was it possible that from these cohesions hierarchies emerged and in eons of crushed blue glass finally concepts of up and down, east and west? Was it simply an inevitability that morality invent itself, the whisper of good and evil just behind a blue shoulder?

"Are you saying yes?" Carlotta McKay demanded. She had been pacing in Brazilian red stiletto heels. She stopped abruptly and brought her pale and dramatically rouged face inordinately close to Diana's. "Blink once for yes," she instructed.

These are the antique corridors, Diana realized, the blue convolutions where grace resides. Here we turn like planets, born and dying alone, isolated by our own light-years. This is where we light the candle and blow the flame out.

Diana Barrington blinked. The action seemed stunning and singular, almost the distillation of all previous methods of discrimination, judgment, and their resolution. It had the complexity and subtlety of whale migration or ballet. And it was blue.

"You were cold yesterday. Are you still cold?" Carlotta McKay inquired. Carlotta stared at her eyes.

Diana Barrington forced herself to blink. In the pale distance, in the blue of debauchery and exhaustion, Carlotta appeared enormous and clear and oddly magnified. She might have been a recently displaced iceberg. She approached with a field of blanket in her arms. She bent down and wrapped a quilt around Diana's shoulders.

"You'll be warm in Nevada," Carlotta told her. "It'll be at least a hundred and ten."

One hundred and ten, Diana Barrington longed to repeat. One hundred and ten severely pointed assertions, but of what? There are only the blue gradations, after all, breaking at your feet like the ten thousand fingers in the imploring hands of a newly formed blue deity. There is only the arrested dusk, after all, and the onrush of the soft blue glistening vagaries, the sanctioned hours and the way one rubs one's mouth.

"You can't just sit on the kitchen floor shivering," Carlotta decided. "Not for six weeks. Mercury, Nevada, will cure you."

"Okay," Diana managed, pushing symbols out of the void of her mouth. "Good," she found the ability to say, developed the method, the sequence of things, the invention of syllables and language. Diana leaned back against the cool enamel walls of her kitchen, drained. She might have fallen asleep, but Carlotta was pacing near her, the garish high heels almost grazing her where she sat wrapped in a quilt on the floor.

"You'll have to get to the Federal Building. You'll have to take a shower, wash your hair, find a sleeping bag, pack food. You'll need a flashlight and canteen. You'll have to make an effort. You'll have to do the rudiments or I'll think you're too sick for this adventure," Carlotta was saying.

Carlotta was studying the gold dial of her wristwatch. The watch came from France. Diana could remember this. The band was made from the skin of some vanishing species of reptile. Was it possible that the dial of her best friend's wristwatch was somehow connected to a temperature matrix? Did this have something to do with the one hundred and ten blue assertions? Were time and climate also a continuum?

"You're going to have to make the effort," Carlotta was telling her, pacing in her incredibly red and sharp spike heels. "I'll bottom-line you. Pack an overnight bag or I'm going to call the paramedics."

Call them, Diana Barrington thought. I'm too sick for this.

"Stand up or I'm dialing," Carlotta McKay said.

Diana stood up. Carlotta McKay was doing something. She was writing down the elements in the required procedure. Each item was given a distinct blue number. She would have to take a shower, put on lipstick, assemble objects in a canvas bag, and drive her car down Sunset Boulevard to Westwood. She would park in the lot behind the Federal Building. Carlotta would find her and help her. Carlotta would sit next to her and read poetry out loud for her. Diana would have to make this effort or Carlotta McKay was going to telephone the police.

"Will you do this?" Carlotta asked, voice soft. Carlotta was staring into the blue grids of her eyes, searching for the implications of communication. "Will you do this for me?"

Blue repetitions, Diana Barrington was thinking, the way water casts a spell across eons of liquid. The way the sea stalls, enchanted. And Kauai, where the Pacific is a slow drugged and electric blue beyond all the distilled clarities. How you return to it like opium. No time has passed. All is forgiven.

"I'm tired of holding my breath," Carlotta McKay informed her.

Carlotta's face was an assemblage of slow blue symmetries. A long time passed before Diana could blink.

They were moving fast through a dark blueness, through the lie of night. Outside the window, the moon was absolutely full, an astonished white. Diana Barrington began to shiver. They were crossing the desert, like Moses and Buddha. They were supplicants without candles. And she would never be warm enough.

"Do you remember where we are going? Or why?" Carlotta asked her.

A blue flash of Rimbaud. A frontier with its provinces still and gutted. It was always a disappointing season. The carnival came, pitched its torn tent, a woman walked a rope above sawdust. The air was an unusual blue, as if prayers had risen from deserted wharves where the idols went blind. The voices of the devout mingled in the paralyzed blue air, torturing it with radiance and handfuls of small flames.

"Do you remember the demonstration?" Carlotta was searching her face. She seemed angry.

Diana shook her head no. There had been a man in the front of the bus. He had done something, but his presence was inconsequential. If he had recited a poem or a psalm or juggled fruits or listed the names of stars and planets, saints, or healing plants, she would have remembered. There had been a man less than a comma in the ocean, a fluid subtraction in the infinite blue text.

"It's a nonviolence demonstration," Carlotta was saying. Carlotta brought her face close to Diana's. "Civil disobedience. We are going to Mercury, Nevada. We are going to shut down the nuclear facility. We may get arrested. We are going to make a statement. Can you remember this?"

Diana shook her head no.

"You know, it's like you are your own nuclear winter," Carlotta mused, "shivering and delirious simultaneously. Your face is ashen. Your pupils are dilated. Are you hallucinating? Is everything still blue?"

You got that right, Diana wanted to say, but couldn't. And then, as if a border in her inexplicable violet interior had been crossed, Diana Barrington recognized that she could speak again. It was the brief blue thaw she was learning to live between.

"Do you think Sartre was right?" Diana asked.

"That hell is other people?" Carlotta said. "Definitely."

"And Shelley? Was Shelley right?" Diana Barrington wanted to know this.

"That prophecy is an attribute of poetry, not vice versa?" Carlotta was staring into her eyes.

"Yes. Exactly." Diana said. She felt breathless. There was so much unusual blueness. It seemed archaic, raw, and elegant. It was the blue of certain beads and pottery: the blue that has been birthed by a kiln; it was the sort of blue that lingered in rooms where the names of gods were called out with adoration. Even Carlotta's eyes seemed moist and blue.

"Yes. Shelley was right," Carlotta said.

"Do you think Pound was right?" Diana pushed a blue flame into the fire of the many-tiered blue night.

"That you owe your audience nothing?" Carlotta asked.

"Yes. Absolutely. Or one cannot but pander. Is this a quiz?"

"Yes," Diana replied.

Diana listened to the sound of her voice. It was sudden and crisp, almost audacious. It might be an intimation of autumnal configurations, structures in the regions of fallen leaves. It occurred to her that the desert floor was clear as a kind of mirror. It might be possible to articulate the universe visually. Or one could stand on the dark stones and look directly into one's heart.

"You're forming sentences again," Carlotta noted. "Look at your mind. Your first words are a quiz." There was something unpleasant in Carlotta's voice.

Diana said, "Yes."

"Is this a desert quiz or a generic survival quiz?" Carlotta seemed amused.

"Yes," Diana answered.

It was a sharp blue yes like a slap. This is where we are born and drown, Diana thought, in the blue channels where there are no directions, no harbors, no one to ring the bells. Steeples have not yet been invented. The people of the region spend their days sleeping. Later, they will drink the indigenous alcohol made from perverse fruits and sing songs of no consequence. In nine months, a crop of lean babies will be born blue and still.

"Your face is quite incredible," Carlotta revealed. "You're on the verge of becoming linguistically impaired again. I can see it coming. Ray Charles could see it coming."

"Yes," Diana managed. She was very cold.

"You have articulate moments. Then it passes and you're frozen again. It's fascinating. Also, you've got a major tic below your right eye now. The entire side of your face is affected. Did you know that? And you're shivering again," Carlotta told her.

"Yes."

"Do you think you'll be drooling soon?" Carlotta asked. "I don't want you to embarrass me with people I may well be jailed with."

Carlotta seemed to be waiting for Diana to extract a reply of some kind, some practical blue form, perhaps, like a species of precocious amoeba. Diana tried to blink and found that she could not.

Diana Barrington wanted to tell Carlotta about the quality of the blue, infiltrating her conventions with wild birds and fluid dialects. There were blue mouths and skies with masked clouds and stars and complicated rituals of tenderness in blue rain. It is my fortieth year and I have come to know distance and blueness. At least I know that, Diana thought. All other geography is false.

After a time, informed by blue grids on which the nuances came and went, Diana Barrington realized that Carlotta McKay was no longer staring at her. In fact, Carlotta was now looking out of the bus window, at the immaculate almost black of the desert and the moon, which was somehow even fuller and a more aggrieved white, a blanched and discarded accomplice.

Diana was considering the implications of the white moon in the fields of night sky when she became aware of a disturbance Carlotta was causing. Carlotta was swaying in her bus seat and snapping her fingers. There was something terrible about this. Carlotta was making the sacred prayed-upon air of the desert night turn neurotic and sordid. Carlotta was adjusting her Walkman radio, pushing the earphones deeper into her ears, and turning the volume up. "I just grew, tangled up in blue," Carlotta McKay sang, aggressively out of tune.

There are forms even in madness, Diana recognized. Even when the self is revealed as tundra, even in the severe and incalculable, the remote arctic of a ravaged interior. Even where the borders have banished themselves and the increments are a mere suggestion, even then there are gestures which are appropriate and those which are not. There is bruised and there is tawdry, Diana decided. And the line must be drawn.

Diana felt desperate and exposed in her seamless avenues of solitude. She looked at Carlotta and felt the horizon expand extravagantly into an exquisite malignancy. The possibilities were exposed, like the one million blue matches of all your imagined orphans.

Diana Barrington leaned closer. She tapped Carlotta on the shoulder. As Carlotta turned, Diana reached out and gracefully, in one motion, removed the headphones from her best friend's ears. Then she unsnapped the radio from the clip at Carlotta's neck and let the machine fall through her fingers, out the open window, onto the desert floor, where it bounced like a hard blue aching flower.

"It's an era before music, I presume," Carlotta said. She seemed resigned. After a silence in which landmasses created themselves and were sculpted by winds, Carlotta began rummaging in her canvas overnight bag. She extracted croissants, apples, a block of chocolate, and cheese. She forced food into Diana's hands.

"Eat," Carlotta instructed.

Diana began to eat. It was always this way, eating at the full moon when the planet turned hungry and festive. The desert floor was a series of blue rudiments, primitive assertions that would later evolve into issues of distinction, of destiny and free will. There would be a blue echo, fading of course, and the soft impression left by one blue mouth.

"Do you want me to read Paz to you?" Carlotta asked, taking out a book from her canvas bag. "In Spanish?"

Diana blinked. Read the part where he sits down to write in a noon the size of time, she thought. Where outside there are the ruins of afternoon.

"Do you remember where we are going? Or why?" Carlotta asked. The desert was a cool dark blue elegance, a remembrance of tile and beads and mosaics, the continuous blue of a drum across the full-moon sand.

Diana shook her head no.

"To close down the nuclear plant? To make a statement? Try to remember," Carlotta said with feeling. Then she began to read.

The Paz words were blue in the almost black of the desert. And the millennium was coming. It was almost here. Now. Diana tilted her face toward the moon, which was an anguish of light in the borderless fields of stars. This is where the wind is born. This is where they fashion direction. This is where they keep the sails.

Diana opened her mouth to speak, but no sound found its way out. She wanted to explain to Carlotta that it was simply a question of blue elements and their uncertain paths and accidental resolution. Or perhaps blue atoms and their combinations. What about the cobalt blue of Carlotta McKay's breast-cancer treatments? Wasn't that the subliminal intuition, the catalyst, the reason they had come? What blue called to them and why respond? Diana Barrington knew. It was the infected blue of acid rain and nuclear winter and cancer treatments and all things where the violated interiors have turned blue, leaking, and contagious.

Diana Barrington was considering the permutations of

damaged blue when the bus stopped in north Las Vegas. From the window, she could see the Las Vegas strip in a meaningless distance, impossible to calculate. The air seemed alien and hostile. The bus had stopped in a casino parking lot. It was a blue pause, like a blue comma in the ocean. Was it supposed to mean something?

"Stand up," Carlotta said. "Pick up your bag and walk off the bus."

Diana stood up. She picked up her bag. Carlotta was wearing tight Bermuda shorts and garishly overdecorated cowboy boots. It looked as if her boots were studded with rhinestone mock bullets. The air against Diana's face was hot and shocked. It was like kissing the wrong person and getting caught. Diana realized there were many other people, dozens, perhaps more. They had also been on the bus.

Someone holding a clipboard and wearing a whistle around his neck was saying something. If it had been significant, if it was a stanza from Neruda, if it had been the details from a page in an anonymous diary truly and wholly written and spoken, Diana Barrington would have recognized it and remembered.

When Carlotta began walking, she followed. There were other people wearing Bermuda shorts and Walkman radios and carrying canvas overnight bags, bedrolls, and guitars. No one else had rhinestone mock bullets on their boots. They were crossing a deserted ashy street. They filed into a large shabby structure that seemed to be abandoned. There was a quality of dense silence.

"It's a church," Carlotta told her. "We sleep here."

Diana felt breathless. Of course, after the struggle in the desert, after the purification by heat, there is always this asylum, the blessed place, where we are anointed.

Diana blinked. She followed Carlotta into an enormous

cool room. Hundreds of small mounds littered the floor. She tripped over one, lost her balance, and fell across another. The mounds were oddly pliant, soft, and she suddenly realized, possibly verbal.

"Jesus, you're stepping all over people," Carlotta whispered. Her voice was harsh.

Diana blinked.

"Can't you see? It's people, sleeping. People from other buses, from other cities. Jesus, I can't go on with this," Carlotta admitted. She had stopped near the altar. She had spread out her sleeping bag. Now she unrolled Diana's.

"Lie down and go to sleep." Carlotta glanced at her watch. "The bus leaves again in three hours."

Diana got into her sleeping bag. Carlotta was staring at her.

"Take your shoes off first," Carlotta said. She sounded disgusted.

Diana blinked. She took off her shoes. She got back into her sleeping bag. The sanctuary was cold and impersonal. One wall was composed of a blue stained glass. The configuration was angular and precise. It was a distillation of remote afternoons spent selecting names for daughters, giving these daughters the names of qualities and jewels, Grace and Faith, Ruby and Jade. It was the blue of prophets and heretics, of the place where abasement and silence mate and are comprehended.

Diana closed her eyes. She thought of the way the ocean looks one hour east of Oahu, when Borneo and Fiji are cousins. She knew she could go there, into the blue dynasties littering the flesh of the Pacific like children. This reef, this matrix, this turquoise interpretation. Or bluer. The blue of all the accommodations.

This is how we live, Diana thought, between these vertical blue intuitions, where Jesus and Buddha walk along avenues of blue glass and burning flowers. And names and divisions have been shed as inadequate. There are only a few random syllables in the universe and they are whispered, holy, holy, holy, holy, blue, blue, blue.

In the morning, on the bus, the sun is almost unbearable. There is an intensity in the sky above her that Diana is attempting to ignore. It is not blue, so it is insignificant. She says, "Can we sleep there again?"

"No," Carlotta replies immediately. "We go back to L.A. after the demonstration. If we're not in jail. I'm afraid St. James of the Fried Cactus or whatever it was happens for you only once, like birth and death. Try to make the best of it."

They are aiming themselves east, farther into the desert. The land is increasingly hot, sparse, insomniac, and fearful. Here the stones dream their blue dreams but do not believe them, Diana is thinking. Perhaps they are fierce dramas informed by lethal intoxications, a violet abscess of grief, the delirium of morning, of wails, of all the lost tokens. You can't tell these dreams at breakfast.

"We're going to make a statement," Carlotta is saying, perhaps to herself. "Do you remember?"

Diana says, "Yes."

She thinks, this is how we part the walls. We do it with our fingers. We walk on sand that burns. We give our flesh for this. We are walking on the burning blue sand, above the perpetual and unceasing drumming. We are opening and closing the millennia of our slow mouths. We are saying up and down, good and bad, right and wrong, yes and no under the clouds.

"I want to ask you something," Carlotta says. She reaches over and removes Diana's aviator sunglasses. Then she removes her own. Their eyes are very close. "I've got a few questions. Before you coalesce or disintegrate, and it's a toss-up, you could do either. Do you know that?"

"Yes."

"I have several questions," Carlotta begins.

"It is always a noon the size of time. It's a matter of blue and its modalities. You are your brother's keeper, always. Jesus saves. Buddha saves. Moses saves." Diana feels her voice. It is steady.

"I want to know what it's like," Carlotta says.

"It's nothing like we thought. Ophelia doesn't play here. You can't sing by the river. There are no rivers or songs here. It's not an abundance but an absence. You don't need your French sunglasses or your tropical wardrobe." Diana is staring at Carlotta now. "You won't be taking photographs or sending postcards. There are no beaches, no mail service."

"Are you going to come back?" Carlotta's voice is soft now.

"I don't know," Diana admits.

"Is there grace and redemption?" Carlotta suddenly asks. Diana laughs. "Always."

"What about my cancer?" Carlotta is staring into her eyes.

Madness. Revelation. The archetypal blue pathways between the nothing. The continuum of knowing. Asylum after struggle. The evolution of an identity suffocating in blueness. Diana looks at Carlotta. There are a billion blue variables between them.

"They got it all. No resurgence. You are clean," Diana replies.

The bus stops. Outside, on the minimalist floor of the desert, where even the rocks seem singular and doomed, thousands of women, children, and men are forming irregular eddies. They are holding paper signs and long paper and cloth banners. Beyond them, beside the line of the fence, hundreds of uniformed police stand shoulder to shoulder. Diana Barrington knows what they are doing. They are guarding the nuclear facility at Mercury, Nevada.

After the obsessions, the absences, the shadows from candles on the avenues of bougainvillea, after the atrocities of blue we invent these barbed-wire lines so we may cross them. We do this in the desert where Buddha walked. We step down from buses into the arms of police with weapons. We do this because we are haunted and sick by the thought of the violet horror of nuclear winter, because of the chill, its permanence. We are born for this, Diana is thinking.

They are standing on the desert now. There are no abstractions. The sand beneath her feet is hot. She can feel her body now and perhaps that is significant. She can feel the sand. The sun. The sun on her back, her face, stinging.

"If you're arrested and can't speak, I'll say you're a performance artist. I'll say you've taken a vow of silence. You won't speak until there is world peace," Carlotta tells her.

Diana blinks. She is thinking that it would be good to not speak until the issues have been resolved, with their pale violet injuries and afternoons of disappointment. And silence through the nights of the pitch blue haunting.

"I'm afraid," Carlotta says.

They are walking toward the fence. The line of police is longer, closer. She can see their weapons where the sun glances off metal. They wear garments of brown and green. They seem specific to the desert, better adapted. She can

almost see herself reflected in the black voids of their sunglasses.

"I'll protect you," Diana says.

"You? You're a poet. It would look terrific on your ré-
sumé." Carlotta sneers. "If I'm arrested, I could lose my
license. I'm an attorney. What about me?" Carlotta's eyes
seem wide open, tight, and wild.

It's okay, Diana is thinking. This is the only blue intox-
icant, the one seduction we are certain we remember. This
is why the journey begins and ends in acres of arrested blue
intensities. This is why we inhabit rooms and landscapes,
why we create harbor lights in autumn and all the virescent
things, even the ambiguous plaza and whispered dialects.
There is only this, Diana Barrington is thinking as they
approach the perimeter of the nuclear facility. There is only
this topography of the heart, with its liquid channels like
rivers of solitude, the rivers of an unnamed world waiting
for love, for definition, for release, for the final blue rain
where the borders dissolve.

Diana takes her best friend's hand. She is beginning to
remember. They are walking across sand now. She opens
her mouth. "No more nukes," she shouts.

"Are you certain?" Carlotta is looking at her. Carlotta's
face is extremely pale. They could reach out and touch the
police.

"Yes." Diana replies. Then, loud, "No more nukes."

The sun is directly over her head now. It is a deliberate
configuration. The sun is a presence, perhaps another fact
in the blue, another entity. This is something she can think
about later. There is now and there is later. There is her
hand and the hand of her friend. There is the glare, the
sun, the metal. There is this walking across wooden boards,
this passing through the wire that once was a fence. There
is this holding of Carlotta's hand and how many others in

this line holding hands, holding banners and signs. They are walking into the ruined blue gash where they manufacture the diseased molecules and atoms and they are saying no. There are things blue and things other and how now and finally she is no longer cold.

FALLING

IN OCTOBER

IT WAS A SATURDAY IN OCTOBER AND SHE somehow found herself at a movie theater on Santa Monica Boulevard in West Los Angeles. She had no idea who the director was, what the film was about, or what the critics had said because she never read anything but poetry written by poets who were dead. On this particular night, Diana Barrington had not been to a movie in at least five years. She was so incredibly ignorant about the culture in general that she was almost in a state of grace.

The film proved to be European. It had subtitles. It was in black and white. Diana Barrington perceived these details as extraordinary. She felt deeply moved and somewhat disoriented.

As she walked toward her car, she was consumed by images of Europe. It is snow I need, she thought, Paris and Berlin and trees like maples and lindens. And Gothic buildings, cathedrals with spires, town squares and rivers and string quartets, cafés and realistic-looking apartments and Rilke. It would be a whole other cadence, a landscape of serious angles and deliberate architecture, religion, and vegetation that was deciduous. It occurred to her that to confront the concept of Europe was to deal with the father, the patriarchy, structure, science, and history. The concept of Europe took her breath away. She began gasping for air.

She felt better once she was in her car with the doors locked. "I am finished with palm trees and mango stands and mother earth," she said out loud, slamming her foot on the gas and driving as fast as she could. "I am through with the elements and cycles. It is Vienna I need, Beethoven, psychoanalysis, and libraries and places where people still smoke and fall in love."

Los Angeles was a shabby little tropical village compared to Europe, with its monuments and substantiality and ornate decadence. The Los Angeles streets looked tawdry to her and pathetically second rate, like some marginal southern fishing town where the bay gradually grew polluted and the population drifted away.

Diana Barrington realized that if she had gone to New York or London or even Calcutta after college instead of home to Los Angeles, her entire life would have been different. She would have filled her poems with traditional images containing obvious medieval associations, steeples and granite arches and recognizable gods and the colors of the Danube and Thames, grays and slates and metals. And the sorts of progressions that defined Western civilization, rather than the random cyclic mutations that were southern California.

She was seized by the compulsion to write a poem. She parked her car near a vacant lot between two low stucco apartment buildings that featured ornaments of some sort near the carports, perhaps the remnants of sundials or coats of arms, if such a thing were possible. "I must have Europe, the Atlantic, cafés, the chill, the brutally cold gray rain falling metallic like bullets," she wrote. "Anything but this unbearable purgatory of turning forty in solitude, in Los Angeles, in October, when azaleas erupt."

Diana Barrington glanced out of the car window. She studied the sidewalk and the thin suggestion of garden near the apartment wall, searching for vivid details. She considered herself a realist, after all. "And there are bird of paradise," she wrote, "and gladiolus and the earth is an indecency, voluptuous and insipid."

That was Los Angeles, she agreed with herself, suddenly shooting out into traffic without looking. Voluptuous and insipid. A stupid woman. Diana Barrington recognized that she should have gone from Berkeley directly east. Instead she had squandered her life beneath these horrid, dull, sun-poisoned palms where anemic black rats lived. This was the homeland of impoverished rodents. And she was finally perceiving Los Angeles stripped of illusions. It was a land of pygmies.

Diana Barrington decided not to tell her six-year-old daughter, Annabell, that they would soon be moving to a major capital where they did not know a single person and could not speak the language. A gray spiked city where the architecture aggressively asserted a premise they could not begin to comprehend. A place where the vegetation, menus, and modes of transportation were alien.

On Monday morning, after she put Annabell on the school bus, Diana drove downtown. She would tell her best friend, Carlotta, that she had at last and definitively recognized the diminutive nature of Southern California, its garish squalor.

Diana began searching for Carlotta's black Jaguar. She drove slowly up and down the ruined side streets offering unrestricted parking in the area surrounding the court buildings. It had been months since Carlotta could afford garage parking. Now Carlotta had to leave her Jaguar unprotected in the glare of daylight while she hiked three quarters of a mile to court in her Italian alligator stilettos.

Diana Barrington experienced a sudden spasm of affection for Carlotta. She appreciated the statement Carlotta was making. Let the IRS garnishee her salary. Carlotta McKay was not going to compromise her fashion imperatives.

Diana considered the possibility that Carlotta McKay might be the only human being besides her daughter that she had ever loved. A best friend had resonance. It was something substantial, as in the ancient times, when there were families, recognizable categories of stable and permanent attachment, like sisters-in-law and godparents. And they had become blood sisters at the right time, before the plague, when such rituals were still plausible.

It was noon. Carlotta was bound to be near the court building. Carlotta no longer ate in her usual restaurants. No one would let her run a tab anymore. She could not get a bowl of rice in Chinatown on credit. She could not even get one alligator stiletto into the door of the Biltmore.

Diana found what appeared to be Carlotta on a bench in a seemingly accidental park two blocks from court. She wasn't sure that it was Carlotta. The woman on the bench looked bloated, awkward, and hunched. Diana approached with caution. It was Carlotta, eating a bag of cheese-flavored tortilla chips. On the bench by her side was a pile of candy bars and a Pepsi. It wasn't even a Diet Pepsi.

Carlotta saw her expression and shrugged. "Sixty bucks a week for food. That's what the IRS allots me," she said with a mixture of sorrow and contempt. Carlotta McKay was bulimic. "Sixty bucks. I used to spend that on break-fast."

They considered her past breakfasts in silence. Diana sat down on the bench, on the other side of the Mars Bars and bags of M&Ms. She averted her eyes from the candy.

"I'm having a moment of clarity," Diana began. She was aware of feeling confused. "I see Los Angeles as it truly is. It's a region of pygmies."

"These jerks need a chair to make a phone call. They're dwarfs," Carlotta McKay immediately agreed. "It's a Toulouse-Lautrec derby. Somebody threw them all down the stairs. Their legs didn't grow."

"One's integrity demands self-exile and Europe," Diana said. Her voice was conspiratorial.

"Europe?" Carlotta McKay laughed. It was a thin, mean sound. "You think it's different there?"

Diana felt stung. "Yes. I certainly do."

"It's a century of pygmies. It's still the Middle Ages. Where have you been? Ignorance, plague, the whims of senile bureaucrats, sadism, and no illumination. You think this is a new age?" Carlotta stared at her. Carlotta had got-ten her hair cut again. It was platinum and extremely short. It looked shaved. It looked obscene and shocking.

"I'm in court all day. I heard some stuff this morning that makes the Crusades look good," Carlotta told her.

"What about bridges with faces carved into them? Art and intricacy? And seasonal variations?" Diana tried. She shut her eyes, hoping she could remember specific details from the film she had just seen. She couldn't.

"Seasonal variations," Carlotta repeated. Her lips curled. "Right." She put a handful of M&Ms into her mouth.

It was clear that Carlotta had jettisoned her diet. She had a heart-shaped face, and every ounce over one hundred and twenty-five pounds went directly to her chin. Yes, the double chin was showing. And Carlotta seemed extraordinarily pale. Diana leaned across the pile of candy to study her face. It was incredible, but Carlotta was not wearing makeup. There were several prominent black hairs along her upper lip. Perhaps Carlotta was eating junk food and also missing her electrolysis appointments. To see Carlotta in the glare of noon was to violate her.

"If you had to choose, which would it be?" Diana heard herself ask. "Berlin? Vienna? Or Prague?"

"Prague?" Carlotta repeated. "You can barely get to Santa Monica."

Diana became aware of something sharp ricocheting through her. It was a sensation she found unpleasant. She was angry with Carlotta. She disliked her attitude, her arrogance and cynicism. She hadn't even had the drama of procuring a passport yet and selecting which cold, angular city to vanish into, and already the European configuration seemed antiquated and false.

She looked hard at Carlotta. "Sometimes I don't think we have a relationship. We're each other's captive audience. We don't interact. We do material. We do routines."

"Life's a routine," Carlotta replied, unscathed. "Or maybe you hadn't noticed."

Diana tried to think of something ameliorating to say. "Remember Monterey Pop? The Summer of Love?"

"I remember," Carlotta told her. "But you weren't there."

"I wasn't?" Diana was shocked by this information. She had vivid and complex memories of this event. In fact, Monterey Pop was a sacrosanct element in her personal mythology.

"You refused to go at the last minute," Carlotta revealed. "You said there'd be no place to park and the bathrooms would be dirty."

They sat in silence. There was a light wind. It occurred

to Diana that it was only the going that mattered. Departures and terminals, the theaters of void. The entire world elongated, the color of a perpetual noon above a suburb between San Francisco and Los Angeles.

Always we are arriving after the journey across the nothing, Diana was thinking. We stand on a balcony or a porch. We say, perhaps here. We can meet on the day when volcanoes mate and the ambience is strident with apocalypse that does not come. We stand on the damp grass beneath an indifferent sunset. And there are no lost ships, no aberrant swaying naked, enraptured, in a corrupted midnight wanton with lies. It is just us, after all, drinking too much with the radio too loud.

"I was thinking about Alex last night," Carlotta said, her voice all at once soft. She was opening a Mars Bar and throwing the wrapping paper to the ground.

Diana felt her eyes widen. It had been years since she had seen so flagrant a display of littering from anyone who had graduated from a UC campus.

"Remember Alex?" Carlotta asked unnecessarily. She was searching her face.

Diana nodded. Of course she remembered Alex.

"I was reviewing our last weekend," Carlotta began. Her voice sounded as if it were detached from her body. She was picking a candy bar apart with her fingernails and throwing pieces of chocolate at the pigeons. Literally. It was clear that Carlotta was aiming at them.

"It was the October just before I got sober," Carlotta was saying. "I kept thinking, I am falling in October, falling in October. I didn't know the streets anymore. I'd drive through West Hollywood and think it could have been Constantinople under a sultry moon in a dangerous season. I felt like I was on acid. Alex and I would tell each other lies for hours. The more extravagant the lie, the more we pretended to believe it. I was convinced he understood me. He knew I was living like a wild dog. He knew I was capable of anything. I could buy a ticket to Maui today. Or Ceylon."

"Or Europe?" Diana offered. Europe was a gray word disappearing into a grainy, unresolved magnitude. It was beginning to lose its clarity and dimension.

"Not Europe," Carlotta corrected. "Europe is too retro. Anyway, I'm picking Alex up at the airport. His plane is late. I'm drinking. Then I'm nervous that I'm loaded. So I go to the bathroom, sniff coke, and put on more makeup. Then I go back to the bar. I've been doing this for five hours. When he finally shows up, he's bombed. We can't find the car. Then we go to the parking lot, sniff more coke, and look for the damn car."

"I don't remember this story," Diana admitted.

"I never told you. Finally, we find the car but I don't have the keys. We tear off a chunk of rail and break the window. There's glass all over the seat. He hot-wires the car. We stop at traffic lights and kiss. The moon is full and red. The moon is absolutely russet. It looks like an ornament, like a distinct entity with a red mouth.

"I feel we've transcended our bodies, outgrown or outsurvived them. When I touch him, my fingers seem to fall through his flesh. My fingers fall through to China or a time before cloth or seasons, when there were only oceans and births and everything burned.

"My apartment is locked. Alex throws a plant through the window and we climb over the terrace. I watched him throw the potted plant and I thought, there are only implements of passion. Everything else is gratuitous. And I kept thinking I wanted to give him a talisman for a god who wouldn't change. Something that would be permanent.

Something insane and drunken, like Kauai at sunset. Something without borders.

"I wanted to be on top, to be able to look down into his face. He was my possession. I wanted him underneath me, on his back, beneath gardenias and fuchsias and all the delicate rarities and expensive intoxications. I looked in the mirror and I was startled. The candles. The red moon. And some crazy glare coming off us. We were in some red zone. It was singular. It was the district I was born for. And my lips were raw from his teeth. I thought, you are why I crossed the ocean, why I stood on the pier and the deserted wharf in rain, wounded.

"We run out of booze around midnight. Alex hot-wires the car. We drive to the liquor store and buy one of everything on my credit card. Brandy. Gin. Tequila. Scotch. Vodka. Kahlúa. We went to the beach. I remember how cold it was. We were in the waves, running and puking and drinking. And he asked me to marry him. I said yes.

"The sun comes up. He's set up an easel in my living room. He's working on a still life. I have to be precise. It was two apples in a white bowl and a lavender rose in a water glass. Bach was on the radio. Alex saw me and smiled. And the air was a rare clarity, as if it was shorn of betrayal, recurrencies, and the tarnished places. I was thinking, painters are right. It is all simply a matter of light and the evolution of sun on petals and flesh. Then he told me he'd met someone else.

"Apparently she had bought a painting from him. She was important in the art scene. He kept repeating that phrase, important in the art scene. It was like he thought he was making an appropriate career move and expected me to appreciate and support that. He said she was gorgeous. He kept saying that, gorgeous. It's not a word you hear much of these days. Then he mentioned that she had a house in the Colony. And a silver Maserati. In her name.

"Her name was Rachel. He would say her name, evoke her name, really, as he listed her many attributes. Rachel of the Peruvian cocaine. Rachel of the French champagne. Rachel of the Russian vodka. Rachel of the Afghanistan hash. It sounded like she had her own private U.N., right there in Malibu.

"I grabbed something. A scissors. I rushed him. And I got him. I cut his shoulder. Blood was spurting out. He's yelling, 'You killed me, you crazy bitch. You killed me.' We embrace. Somebody's called the cops. They show up with an ambulance. We're in each other's arms on the floor. There's glass everywhere from the terrace window we broke to get in. And we're kissing in the ambulance.

"Later, I see him sneaking off to the phone booth. I figure he's calling Rachel. There's no way I'm going to leave. I've got to see her. I may get arrested, but I'm not leaving voluntarily. Finally, she shows up. She's dressed for tragedy. She's thrown a Fendi sable over her aerobic pants. She's got the Jourdan pink satin pumps. She's got the blond hair down to her ass in a shade of ash you cannot even buy in Los Angeles.

"And I'm still a lunatic. I'm following them out to the parking lot. I've paid to see the last card. I'm calling. I don't care what it costs. I've got to see if she's got the silver Maserati. I'm tracking them by her perfume. It smells like genetically engineered mangoes and money and what you imagine a concubine leaves on the sheets." Carlotta leaned against the bench and smiled.

"Did she have it?" Diana wanted to know.

"What do you think?" Carlotta was still smiling.

Diana would like to tell Carlotta what she thinks. But she

cannot even begin to formulate a concept of where to begin.

"You know what I think?" Carlotta asks instead. Diana does not reply immediately. She watches Carlotta stand up. Carlotta is lopsided because of the way her heels have worn down. She can barely balance her body. Diana is struck by Carlotta's ease with savage juxtaposition, how she continues to hike downtown without a credit card or garage parking, refusing to lower her standards or admit defeat.

"What do you think?" Diana asks reluctantly. She senses she doesn't want to know.

"It was the best weekend of my life," Carlotta replies, and walks out of the park.

Diana walks to her car. As she drives west, she thinks of the population with their tiny bodies and monumental, confused appetites. Everywhere, they are having grotesque love affairs and awakening to unprovoked and irrevocable betrayals. They are limping in the skins of endangered reptiles. They are giving each other marriage proposals as conversational filler. In between, they demand acts of consequence and gestures you don't return from.

Diana stops at an intersection. In the street and on the sidewalks are aliens, schizophrenics, drug addicts, criminals and their attorneys, students, housewives, shoppers, borderlines, and tourists. They are the divorced, the abandoned, the broken and disappointed. They are the overstimulated. Some are driving $80,000 automobiles. Grandmothers deliver packages to hoodlums for cash. Children are being gunned down, infants and pregnant women. Plague victims ride in the medical-building elevators. We are supposed to pretend we don't notice. We are supposed to remember our manners. They are counting on this. And it occurs to Diana Barrington that this is a cadence she knows with tenderest intimacy. She doesn't need subtitles. This is a dialect in which she is absolutely fluent.

As she drives down Beverly Boulevard, she is aware of all the women and men standing at windows, on balconies and terraces. Their mouths are small illuminations. Their mouths are wells of death. They are saying, I am your autumn. I am the reason you collect thunder. Paint my body with perfume. Pour rum on me.

Everywhere, from vacant lots and alleys, she can hear the dialogue rising. They are saying, I am your opium and the way you sleep. I am the edges of rooms and landscapes, the harbor lights amber in autumn. You need not cross an ocean. I am Bali and Barcelona and all the boulevards embossed by green assertions and the wind that seduces. I am your ravens, your bronzes, your cared for where night opens soft.

Diana Barrington is breathless with affection. We are all pygmies now, she realizes. We are what is left after the world shrinks. In Berlin and Paris and Los Angeles. She can decipher the words this late-afternoon autumn air speaks. Everywhere women stare at men with eyes the size of fall. These men are standing across a room, balancing jackets on one shoulder like gangsters. Night is a violet danger.

Carlotta is right. It might as well be the thirteenth century. Communication is an abstraction. The city is walled and the bricks are falling. We are besieged by charlatans and thieves. We trade rumors. We practice voodoo. We keep plates of chalk and salt near us, for protection. We hang strands of garlic and recite mantras. We are intimate with the details of possession. We wear cowrie shells, crosses, crescents of moon. We dip satin in cologne to please deities from Africa. We wear rocks and crystals. We carry tiny Buddhas. We carry condoms. We carry cash and concealed weapons. We carry affirmations and emergency telephone numbers. We carry passports. We carry the Hazelden meditation series. We keep altars with objects that fascinate and repel us.

It is still the Dark Ages. And we are too small for our lives. Spider monkeys and langurs are doing better. At least they live in troops. They protect infants and share food. They groom each other. We stay home, by ourselves, locked in our apartments. We do calisthenics until we sprain our ankles. We eat sixty-dollar breakfasts and deliberately throw them up. We rent twelve videos and buy a box of chocolate chip cookies and go home alone. We cannot remember living differently. We can barely remember morning. It's the tedium, the brain damage, the blackouts, the stress, the acid flashbacks, the armed robberies and earthquakes. And there are no nervous breakdowns anymore. No one gets to go to bed for six months anymore. The best you can get is an episode. They expect you up on your feet after a weekend. You go until you drop. Now it's the risk factor. We tremble at the thought of who and what is out there. We are afraid to look out our windows. We are motionless in our beds. We can remember when we caught bass and halibut from the Santa Monica pier.

Now we don't even watch television anymore. We don't even masturbate. Some of us have stopped dieting and going to our electrolysis appointments. We deliberately litter. We make a conscious decision to start smoking again. We gamble. We starve and binge and purge. Our teeth are falling out. The porcelain is peeling off. And in the street, there is a sense of the limitless dark scented with lemons, oranges, adobe, and sagebrush. The air is ancient, sharp, and malicious. It was here first.

It's been the Day of the Dead for a thousand consecutive years. We know this and we are paralyzed. In between, we want too much. There is the inevitable detox. And disappointment that feels like a gash inside the eyes or a nest of trapped birds, depraved, wild with malaria. Why not? It's almost the millennium and malaria is making a comeback. And we are depraved, wild with emotional malaria. It's the drugs, of course, though we suspect it is worse. We are searching for signs of the death rash on our lunch break. We have always suspected we were flawed, not really human, somehow terminal and monstrous. Now this.

Diana Barrington parks in her carport in the savaged flats of Hollywood. She is waiting for the school bus to bring Annabell home. Annabell is in the first grade. She is learning cursive writing, French, computer, spelling, soccer, and the principles of nutrition. Europe as a destination has vanished. Los Angeles is a ruined fishing village. Los Angeles is a resort outpost in the Dark Ages. There are only lateral movements. It's a tropical nightmare. There is the torn green of the palms and, eventually, the monotony of the carbon cycle.

It is October and we are falling, Diana Barrington thinks. We are falling in and out of love without warning. We are asking strangers to marry us. The rain is falling like green bullets or the accelerating glass we have been watching for, the glass bullets of bombs and earthquakes. We are falling to the ground, through the earth itself, into debt and disaster. We are small and defective and the walls of our cities are falling. Our satellites are falling, chunks of metal fall from the lesions of the sky, from our illusionary channels of communication. We have nothing to say and the metal is a kind of rain. And we are falling off the wagon. We are falling down drunk. We are falling down stunned. We are falling from grace. We are falling in October and they can't catch us all. We are falling because there is no more gravity.

The laws of the universe no longer apply to us. We are like leaves, only smaller. It is our season to come apart.

In the unpunctuated dark we are trembling violently. People without homes or food sleep on our lawns, in our cars. Many have lost their minds. They don't have shoes. Their feet are black. Has tar congealed on them? Is it gangrene? They don't look American. We step over them. We suspect everything is contagious at this point, and they are not telling us.

We are alone. We even have our babies alone, like contaminated animals. We barely manage not to eat them. Baboons seem sophisticated. Compared to the complexity of primate social interactions with their behaviors of affection and tolerance, we are primitive. We possess a grief so encompassing that to admit it would require immediate suicide. We raise these infants alone. We teach them to love with their teeth. We teach them to make Molotov cocktails and face the tanks. You can put that one in the bank.

In between, we make terrifying promises to one another. He says, Abandon yourself to the possibilities. She removes her skin.

In between, we stand in the new lover's bathroom. His necessities are displayed. The beast cannot possibly be this nasty or need this many products to contain it. We learn more about him by opening cabinets than he will ever tell us.

We live by the revelations of objects and what they imply. He needs toothpaste, dental floss, plaque remover, shaving lotion, razors, antacid tablets, fiber laxatives, deep-heating lotion, throat spray, cold-sore gel, saline solution, sterile pads, hair dye, acne cream, baby lotion. There are more shelves but we have seen enough. We are dizzy. There is absolutely no way that we are going to buy into this.

Six months later we test negative. We celebrate by going

to hotels and meeting in lofts in delirious combinations in afternoons without edges. We know it is forbidden. But we can't help ourselves. We are enacting Haitian rituals and reciting Tibetan prayers. Some of us are sober. We are going to AA. We are carrying lucky charms and stilettos. We are desperate. We are keeping candles lit because we are becoming afraid of the dark.

In between, we sin, we transgress. We always thought there should be a punishment for what we do with our bodies. We always thought we should be put to death for this. Now some of us are. And we can't believe we have done it again. After we promised. And we don't know if we can stop on a consistent basis. We grew up in the sixties. There was nothing penicillin couldn't cure.

In between, we are calling the paramedics. We are having convulsions and heart attacks. We are putting fantastic mixtures of powders and potions into our noses and lungs and veins. We are staging garish infidelities where we sweat and moan and heave and pant and silently count to ten thousand and no one gets off. We just don't want to be taken alive.

In between, we are walking out of motels, closing the door behind us, saying *that* never happened. We are waking up in a cold sweat, wondering if last Saturday night is actually going to kill us. We are saying it's just a bit of indigestion, locking the bathroom door and rocking back and forth on the cold tiles, shaking. We have to wait six months for the next blood test. We spend it at home, alone, with the door locked. We have to keep ourselves in.

Then we are racing to airports and throwing bricks through windows. We are getting into limos and company jets, river rafts and horse-drawn cabs. We are kissing in the broken glass. We are taking the psychiatric medication. We are taking the twelve-foot waves. We are stepping over the dispossessed to get into private clubs where we pogo, throwing off our shoes and pulling out splinters without missing a beat. The moon is russet. The air is red. We are rushing each other with scissors and knives. We are having the time of our life.

VIRGIN OF
TENDERNESS

MAGGIE DECKER HAS ALWAYS WANTED
to fall off the world as it is ordinarily known and it seems
she has finally done it. She is looking at icons in the crypt
beneath the Church of Alexander Nevsky on Ruskie
Boulevard in Sofia. She pauses in front of the Virgin of
Tenderness, noting how abstract and isolated she seems.
She is insulated by a background painted with a pigment de-
rived from lapis lazuli. Half a millennium later the color
is undamaged. It glares like a permanent blue truth. The
Virgin of Tenderness has a garish silver hand. She has been
kissed by so many that parts of her body have been covered
with a protective metal.

"Did you see the Virgin of Tenderness?" Maggie asks.

"No. I'm blind," Heather answers. And, after a moment,
"Of course I saw it. You always ask the worst questions."

Maggie is quiet as they climb marble stairs. She pauses

in the chapel to light a candle for her daughter. Bless her in her cynicism, she thinks, and her aggressive ignorance.

Then they are sitting in the car again and the chauffeur is taking them out of the city. There are yellow trollies on boulevards bordered by dead birch and oak. She can see snow on the Balkan Mountains beyond the Palace of Culture. The gold dome of the Church of Alexander Nevsky is behind them. They are passing empty parks with dismissed chestnuts and bronze soldiers on horseback. There is the soft red fluttering of communist flags above cobblestones. It is late winter. The sun seems distant and flat.

She studies her daughter's face. Heather has black hair and creamy pale skin. Her cheeks are the color of apricots. When the sun strikes her hair, it becomes shades of brown and red like the tones of certain polished woods. She thinks of violins and cellos and the music lessons Heather took when she was seven. Even then she had a temper.

"You're staring again," Heather accuses.

"It gives me pleasure to look at you," Maggie says.

"It's always about you," Heather replies. She's been waiting for this. "But *you* are making *me* uncomfortable."

Maggie wills her head to turn and it does. The suburbs of Sofia are behind them. Everything is behind them, the Ottoman Empire, the German occupation, the way the Greeks and Romans came. Even the Turks who stayed for five hundred years, smoking hash and playing with themselves, are finally gone.

They are passing mining villages with brick town houses on ruts of dirt streets. The land seems unadorned. Donkeys pull carts. Sheep walk the shoulder of the road like a form of punctuation, something in the margin one could forget to mention. They are on the road to the Rila Monastery. There are occasional patches of snow. A sudden herd of bulls passes. Below are hillsides where apples and walnuts will later grow.

They are parked near the entrance to the compound. The air is sharp with implications, angels and gray devils with the cool sheen of reptiles are painted on ceilings and arches and the edges of balconies. These are the creatures of fever and dream and a severity of winter. This is why they have wound up mountains through a density of birch and chestnut. She opens the door for her daughter.

"My feet hurt," Heather tells her. "You go."

"But you'll never have another chance to see Rila," Maggie says.

"Is that a promise?" Heather is staring at her with contempt. She lights a cigarette with slow deliberation. "I hope I'm never within two thousand miles of this ugly backward country for the rest of my life."

"Heather, please," Maggie Decker begins. She is always beginning.

"You go. I know what's there. They're selling pieces of the saints. They've got their bones in carved filigree boxes. Jesus, this is worse than Mexico."

Maggie Decker walks alone through Rila, past the old women selling bones of the saints in small wooden boxes. She studies an altar cross said to contain six hundred separate carved figures in scenes from the New Testament. It took the monk twelve years to carve. Maggie makes the mistake of asking the tour guide what happened to the monk.

"He went blind on the day it was finished," the guide replies.

"Of course," Maggie says, in English. "What else?"

Then they are passing illuminated manuscripts in Cyrillic, royal decree scrolls with gold seals, and six-foot wooden candles donated by Turkish sultans. There are carved chalices and Russian shrouds with raised figures woven with gold and silver fibers, with gems and pearls for emphasis. It is a tiered world and the skies and underground are also filled.

When she returns to the car, Heather is smoking. She tosses the cigarette out the window, onto the snow. "This place is even worse than I thought," Heather tells her. "This has got to be the country from hell." Then Heather closes her eyes and pretends to fall asleep.

Maggie Decker does not look at her daughter. She does not reach out and touch her arm. She does not speak. The road feels south, even with your eyes closed, she decides. You can feel the drift.

After a time she notices the skeletons of grapevines planted between apartments along a river. There is a snowstorm. Then there are factories and towns without names beside train tracks.

A cold drizzle begins. It is late afternoon in Melnick near the Greek border. Peasant women bend over tobacco. They have passed through the Bulgarian wine country in rolling valleys below mountains with snow. Goats push up hillsides. She is drawn to the sudden yellow of leaves in a gully by a fast-moving stream. It is a stasis of winter. Only russet and orange, red and brown and gray are permitted.

They walk through the town. Heather always walks ahead of her. The town is mostly stone houses with broken porches on which white gourds hang. There is radio disco in subterranean cafés that look dark and gouged as caves.

They sit on a wall Romans built. It is all a matter of suggestion, she thinks. The ruins of a thousand-year-old mineral bath are below them. It is all stone upon stone, one at a time, relentless as cells, she is realizing. And stone is the DNA of the exterior world. And doesn't man build dimensional metaphors of his interior, obsessively constructing what he only subliminally recognizes? And it occurs to Maggie Decker that you can know yourself absolutely in any ancient ruin.

Maggie remembers her daughter at seven. How she would sit on her lap in the morning before school. How she would brush her hair. Or the way they would look into one another's eyes when they spoke. Now she tries to explain the historical significance of the site to Heather.

"Oh, be quiet," her daughter says, annoyed. "History is just the way you try to contaminate me. History is your private excuse. This is not about the Romans."

"What is it about?" Maggie wants to know.

"It's about your petty failures and fear of death." Heather turns away.

Maggie Decker considers her daughter's concept of history. They are driving through trees. These are the woods you don't picnic in but survive, she decides. And it seems she is watching the world through branches, through hillsides of stark crucifixions. And there is only stone and oak and the way bark is between late snows, bark like charred wood when its skin is carved away, when it rises into the cold air waiting to be born.

She wakes up in the middle of the night in Plovdiv, the city she has added to their itinerary because her grandmother was born there. It is raining. She has dreamed about the hospital again, specifically the radiation treatment. She has dreamed she is strapped to the metal table, the invisible rays are entering her body. She can feel them. They are blue and cold like the distilled essence of some profound evil.

Later she watches the day assemble itself from her hotel window. She notes the first random truck, the first taxi and then another. She has spent her life watching cities she is merely passing through wake up. It never meant anything and she wonders, vaguely, why she has adhered to this empty ritual. Outside it is a cold gray falling into the river, the buildings and air.

In the elevator a man says, "There are still forbidden zones in Russia."

"Don't be absurd," the woman with him answers in French. "That is obvious propaganda."

Then they are driving through Plovdiv and the city seems old and bloody, ancient and infected. They are passing streets of low apartment houses beyond the gray river in the sharp gray air.

"Grandmother walked from this city," she tells Heather. "She walked carrying an infant to Antwerp."

Heather doesn't hear her. Heather has a cassette player with earphones on her head. She listens exclusively to punk rock. She writes one postcard after another. It does not seem possible she can know that many people. She avoids even a stray glance out the window.

Maggie Decker had planned to find her grandmother's neighborhood and somehow pay her respects. She has maps and documents with lists of names and reference numbers. But now she decides it is not possible to navigate this density of gray. There are no gestures from her time and region that can apply here.

They have crossed the river. There are flatlands between mountains. She starts to say it could be Northern California, Salinas, perhaps, in winter, but Heather has the earphones on. They are passing a town where clothing has been left to dry on apartment balconies. Snow falls across the sheets. The side streets are the color of leaves. The houses are brick behind a veil of what could be fog or chimney smoke. Everything is the tone of winter and rock and a God who would be hard, severe with his delineations.

In her hotel room, she notices that she is bleeding. There is a moment when she almost faints but she doesn't. She washes her underwear. She dreams of the radiation treatment again. They are staying in a hotel in the Balkan Mountains. She dreams of the hotel. In this dream, she has become the Virgin of Tenderness. She is draped in blue and her hand is a kind of metal hook. She waves her hook at the doctor and says, "It's still winter in the mountains. In the towns, it's still the Middle Ages."

At breakfast, Heather orders wine with her eggs. She drinks in slow motion, letting their eyes meet. "I went to a disco last night," Heather reveals. "And no one would dance with me."

Have your cruelties become apparent, even to strangers? Maggie wonders. Can they sense your callous indifference? She is interested. At last, she asks her daughter why.

"Because I'm from Los Angeles. They know we've got the plague. They were afraid of catching something." Heather pauses. She looks at the ceiling. "This country sucks," she says finally.

Later they are winding into the mountains, into a blizzard, and the car is skidding. They slide onto the shoulder, crashing into branches. This catches Heather's attention. She removes her earphones. Oak trees along the road look solemn and crocheted. They seem frozen in midstep, in some autistic repetition. In this protracted moment they calibrate the movement of stars and who can say what they know or why they chose to point that way at the road? Maggie tells the driver to wait. She can see a small church.

"Why are you going in there?" Heather shouts.

"I want to light candles," Maggie tells her. She is walking.

"You've been lighting candles since Sofia," Heather says. "Is it a new addiction?"

"I wouldn't worry about that," Maggie says. "You need all the illumination you can get."

She is walking and the snow is deeper than she imagined. She steps in past her knees. She can sense Heather behind her now. She can hear her daughter, the car door shutting and some rustling of fur in snow.

The chapel is carved wood and gilt, gilt thrones and icons with metal hands and metal halos. There are Oriental carpets on the stone floor which bears the scars from past fires. Plastic roses in vases rest on the altar beneath icons. Maggie buys ten candles from an old woman with a black birthmark on her cheek.

She stands near the carved wood on the side of the church. Everything is carved in this country, as if men sat in a trance through perpetual winters, playing with knives. Two peasants pass near her and retreat into shadow. They look like movie extras. They have faces lifted from nightmares. They carry the props of bit players, berets and canes and candles and pipes. They dress entirely in black. They have brilliant eyes. Perhaps this is where the grandmothers go to die, she thinks, in Balkan mountain villages where they whisper over brandy while it snows. They stand near the entrances of compounds with thick ankles in black socks and they make sweeping motions at the illusionary ground. It is even possible that her grandmother is already here, waiting for her.

"Are you okay?" Heather asks. They walk in silence across the snow, back to the car. Now Heather looks worried.

"I was dizzy for a moment," Maggie says, suddenly frightened. She is about to tell Heather about the blood. She bites her lip and doesn't.

"It's always something with you," Heather says. Her tone is bitter.

"Why are you so angry?" Maggie studies her face. "Is it about your father?"

"Dad?" Heather's eyes are fixed. "They buried the Dead Hippie in 1969. Then you carried the corpse around for twenty years."

"What else?"

"Your style," Heather tells her. "It offends me. How you stand center stage and suck up all the air. All that drama with the drugs and the paramedics and rehabs. Then the high ritual you turned AA into. Every meeting was opening night. Now this." Heather looks out the window.

The car is moving into the snow. It seems as if the snow is throwing itself against the windshield. It looks purposeful, capable of intention and malice. And they are leaving the mountains behind them. Sheets are drying on apartment balconies as snow falls. There is more brick and stripped trees, streams and wooden fences and the carcasses of grapes.

She dreams she is cold and something blue is forcing its way into her body. She could stop this, but her hands are encased in metal and she has no thumbs. It is an invasion of subtle disguised particles. She wakes up with a start and they are parked in front of the hotel in Turnovo.

It is late afternoon. Maggie wants to see the ruins of the city now. She was spent her life waiting and there can be no more deferments. She knows this. She is walking up a hill, picking her way through rocks and weeds and walking through one of the walled entrances with its remnant of a drawbridge. The river is below. The country is the color of ruins, mustard yellow, brick red, and gray. Somehow the land, the rock and air have coalesced into these lost monuments.

The afternoon is darkening and the bus loads of Russian tourists have left the walled ruins. The plump women with dyed blond hair and bad skin and poorly fitting dull clothing are gone. Below are hillsides of houses, one upon another, a uniform white. The orange roofs seem part of the earth. There is a truth in all this that she can't quite grasp. In the narrow stone and mud streets of Turnovo, men and women wear brown coats and carry loaves of round bread.

Maggie Decker is alone in the ruins of Turnovo. Heather is far below, at the drawbridge, sharing her cassette player with the chauffeur. Nothing moves in the hills or on the river. Maggie reads a description of the annihilation of this city by the Turks in the fourteenth century.

Perhaps because it is winter and almost night and she is alone in these ruins, the idea of what it is to live in a walled city suddenly becomes clear to her. To dwell here would be to live in the only enclosure of civilization in hundreds of savage miles. How unlikely it would be that one would ever reach another city, a Constantinople or Athens. It seems almost impossible to take such a journey, even now.

Maggie Decker considers what it is to be invaded and to have your city burned. It is to erase you and your ancestors from the earth absolutely. There is nothing on microfilm. You and your history, your gods and poetry and children are utterly gone and gone forever. The fall of your city is the fall of the world.

"But you don't know you have a recurrence," Heather points out at dinner. She finishes a second bottle of wine. She glares at her mother.

"No, I don't know absolutely," Maggie agrees. It is important for Heather to believe that she doesn't know. So Maggie does not tell her intoxicated daughter about her intuition or dreams, or how she can feel it growing and spreading. She can feel it moving through her body the way you can feel a shadow across your skin. She doesn't tell Heather about the blood. She turns her eyes away from the wine bottle.

Later she lies in the darkness of her hotel room. Four men are playing cards in the hallway, arguing in Russian. She can hear the church bells, the many bells of Turnovo breaking the night with surgical precision, slicing the hours in half with the inevitability of centuries of slow winters, icons and stone churches, nights they invented vodka for.

Finally there is dawn with its terrible chill, with its icy rivers and bridges and stones. The old world moves in tortuous small circles and goes nowhere. It's been in a coma for a thousand years. You can barely recognize the forms beneath the rain and stupor, beneath the socialist art, gigantic and brain dead. And there are always the church bells with their ugly repetitions, their interminable chorus of gray.

Between Turnovo and the Black Sea, Maggie Decker cannot help but consider her life and the wrong turns that deposited her in this car with the daughter who despises her and the driver who is no longer even bothering to offer suggestive gestures with his lips or fingers. On the streets, whole segments of the population look tainted. There is a ghastly sense of irrevocable winter and a squalor that seems almost intrinsic. They are driving through a city. All the women's coats are either black or brown or navy blue. Spring will never come to this region.

"This is a country where the female orgasm is unheard of," Heather observes. She says this and puts the earphones back on.

The mountains are behind them now. Of course the road is a borderline between time. This country has a tradition of blind singers in marginal areas. Nothing is accidental. It is a country of apple trees and symbols like all others. Now there is a hillside with blue beehives in the snow. A deer the color of blanched leaves regards them by a riverbank.

We come to bring flowers to apartments where our grandmothers once lived. We drive through streets they walked on, but they are dead and their memories are gone and the streets belong to someone else. We journey to abstract ruins. The stones are serene in their insignificance. We are the more wounded.

Heather sleeps and allows herself to slide against her mother, this woman who sits at the center of all drama, taking up the air. Heather sleeps with her head on her mother's shoulder and it occurs to Maggie that it will be easier for her daughter to breathe soon. Now, because she is asleep, Maggie dares to brush her lips against the cheek which is the pink of the sides of apricots in July. She closes her eyes and breathes in the smell of Heather's hair, how forested it seems, how of damp moonlight and some essence of mahogany.

The driver has stopped. The cessation of movement wakes Heather, who bolts upright. They have stopped because the Black Sea is below them. It is a pale blue. Maggie experiences a sharp disappointment.

"What were you expecting?" Heather is regarding her with contempt. "Some real dark drama? I can read you like a book."

Indeed, Maggie Decker thinks. The dénouement is coming and ten to one you don't even know it.

Then they are driving down to the Black Sea port of Varna. She can see the ocean liners with their Russian flags, the cruise ships with the tourists from Moscow. The sun smells fresh.

They walk through the Roman ruins in Varna. When the baths were built, in the second century, the city was called Odessos. She starts to tell this to Heather and then remembers that Heather does not care. She does not believe that the fall of your city is the end of the world, that you are scratching with stone into dirt again. You are naked. You are an animal again and fear the night and the stars and the rain and predators. There are wild cats and sea gulls and the afternoon seems simultaneously ancient and possible. The sounds of haunted seabirds ricochet against the walls. After the fall of the world there are still seabirds.

"Is this it?" Heather asks.

Yes, this is it, Maggie thinks, but says nothing. You sit on a wall where the stones are the color of air in a light sun. From certain angles they seem invisible. You could almost walk through them. Then Maggie remembers there is one more town, Nessebyr. She tells the driver to take them there.

The Black Sea is a gauze below them, a pale restrained blue to the right. It could be the Santa Monica Bay of her youth. She went there with her brother. They would fish for halibut from the pier. If they found enough glass soda bottles to return, they could buy food. The bottles were two cents apiece. Most of the time, there was only enough for one hot dog or donut. Her brother would split the food with her, even though he was bigger. Sometimes they found enough bottles to take the bus back home. Other afternoons they would walk.

Now there are peach trees in a ravine off the road, yellow blossoms on a bush, and a carpet of sheep beneath trees near train tracks. It seems that the sun should set, it's seemed that way for hours, but it doesn't.

There are peach trees in flower. The forests are stripped. The sides of the road are thick with sheep the color of ruins and leaves and air. There is a sense of bells and Nessebyr.

Maggie knows it is the last stop on this awful journey. This is the last walled city Romans built that they will see. She is suddenly hungry and buys cakes from a street vendor. She eats as she walks. She stops to buy shell necklaces from a little boy. She puts them around her neck, one string then two more. She winds a string around her wrists and ankles. She intuits this is necessary. It is still afternoon.

It seems that Nessebyr is on an island. They have crossed a kind of bridge. She is walking on cobblestones. The cottages along the sea are wood and stone and like any beach resort, deserted in winter. She notices small sailboats below her. There are round piles of tiny clam shells in the ancient winter sand.

She has been sitting on the wall of a tenth-century church. There is the constant dialogue of seabirds in the ruins near her. Below and behind her, she can see the bridge they crossed. On the other side of that thin channel is a blue haze and what might be the twentieth century.

She wants to put her hands in the Black Sea. She walks across the sand, bends down, and knows instantaneously what this blue is. This is the blue of prophecy and she can correctly decipher it at last. This is the blue she has dreamed of, what she must anoint her face with.

The rocks are behind her. It is good to think of the world this way, as rock and wood and sand and flat sky and blue water. They raze your city and you are a baboon again. Small quiet-seeming boats with sails are in the water. Tree branches reach out from the shore. There is nothing more.

Maggie Decker is beginning to understand why the Virgin of Tenderness is depicted with lapis lazuli. It is the particular blue of this gulf. She could open her mouth and breathe faith in. There is so much air. It is incredible, but the higher the water touches her, the more clarity and knowledge she is given. She could swim past the stray fishing boats to the breakwater, or even beyond. Her feet can no longer touch the bottom. She can still see Heather standing on the far side of the bridge. It is a construction into a different millennium. Of course time is fluid. If Heather were to cross the bridge, two thousand years would pass. But Heather could never cross it fast enough.

THESE
CLAIRVOYANT
RUINS

SHE WAS AWARE OF A CHANGE IN HER
personal climate. She could feel the edges. They were driving on Melrose Avenue to Annabell's violin lesson. It was her last lesson before her performance in the annual December school pageant, *Fiesta de las Luces*. The Santa Ana winds had blown themselves out. A version of winter had appeared. The cold air seemed to spark against her face. On the trees, the oranges looked icy and metallic.

It had been overcast all week. The sky was completely gray today, enclosed, like a thing not yet born. There was a sense of the sun slowly asserting itself. It seemed to rise from the ground, from beneath the clouds, defying the ordinary. The gray slate of sky seemed illuminated from within, lit by some form of intelligence, perhaps.

"Look at the sunset," Diana said. She could see it behind her, in the rearview mirror. It looked as if the sky was giving birth to continents and islands, land bridges, rain forests, and rivers.

"Why should I? Who cares? The sunset is boring," Annabell replied.

"But this is utterly unique," Diana explained. "L.A. rarely has sunsets like this. This looks Hawaiian. The entire sky is magenta, turquoise, and orange. Sunset in Los Angeles is normally squalid. This, on the other hand, is magnificent."

"Magnificent," Annabell mocked, reproducing her tone. "Like I should care."

"Look at the sunset, goddamn it."

"I'm looking," Annabell lied.

"You're facing east. You can't see it that way. It's behind us. Here. I'll stop the car." Diana pulled the car over to the curb.

Annabell was in the backseat. She did not move a muscle. "All you care about are your stories and poems," she accused.

Diana Barrington felt stung. "That's unfair," she finally decided.

"It's true. My life stinks," Annabell added.

"You are being a brat," Diana realized. Her voice was steady.

"No. I'm not. You're a bad mother, you're a bad mother." Annabell sang this like an advertising slogan.

"You are being hateful," Diana pointed out. She felt she was losing ground.

"You would be, too, forced to drive around in this ratty old car and take violin lessons. The chic thing is piano. I don't even want that silly thing in my life," Annabell informed her. She crossed her arms at the elbow and placed them over her chest.

The violin had cost two hundred dollars. Diana Barrington had borrowed the money. She owed money all over southern California. There were entire neighborhoods she was afraid to even drive through. She could not go to Pasadena, Sherman Oaks, or Venice. After the violin purchase, she could no longer dare Santa Monica. And Annabell had begged for the instrument. She had promised, on her knees, to respect and adore it.

Diana studied her daughter's face. Annabell's mouth was tight, her eyes were evasive and remote. Suddenly Diana felt herself reach out. She struck her child on the arm.

Annabell was stunned. Her eyes softened and enlarged. She opened her mouth. "I'm so sorry," Annabell said. "I don't know what got into me."

"Get out and look at the sunset," Diana Barrington ordered.

"I'm moving," Annabell assured her, and she was. They stood on the sidewalk together.

"I'm sorry I hit you," Diana said, after a moment. They were standing in front of a boutique with enormous dressed-up stuffed animals in the display windows. A five-foot panda wore a white sweater and red silk scarf. A polar bear was dressed in a vest embossed with green-and-violet reindeer.

"It's okay," Annabell said. "I forgive you."

"I'm having a rough time," Diana Barrington began.

"Are you missing Carlotta?" Annabell is all business. "It is time to go the cemetery?"

"Yes. And it's painful. Christmas unhinges me. I gain twenty pounds between Thanksgiving and New Year's. Now there's your recital. I'll have to interact with other mothers. They abhor me." Diana felt the cold air in her face.

"It's because you're not married. You scare them," Annabell offered. She smiled at her mother. "I was a brat. I admit that. It's because I'm insecure."

"About what?" Diana felt her heart stop.

"About everything. How I don't have a father." Annabell stared at her with intensity.

"God." Diana sighed. "Let's walk."

"But I don't have a father. I never even met him," Annabell reminded her. They were walking. Diana was carrying the violin case.

"Having a father can be overrated. I had a father. Trust me. I know," Diana told her daughter.

"What was it like?" Annabell seemed interested.

"I watched thousands of sporting events. Baseball, football, basketball, even some aberrant hockey games and car races. Then there were the occasional boxing matches and the nightmare of the Olympics. I pretended I cared. I memorized batting averages and rushing yards, divisions, postseason play potentials. I had a number I could phone in Las Vegas for the spreads," Diana remembered.

"Why?" Annabell looked at her.

"So we could have something to talk about. He certainly wasn't going to learn the details of anything specific to me. So I contrived to make intelligent conversation about the games. It was the most tedious thing in my life." Diana studied the evening air, as if expecting something.

"What happened?" Annabell asked.

"On Superbowl Sunday, 1979, my father committed suicide. I made maybe three million ham and cheese sandwiches at halftimes, brought them out on trays with bottles of beer. I did this for decades. Then he blew his brains out and didn't leave me as much as a postcard." Diana and Annabell were walking into the early evening on Melrose Avenue. "But the real kicker," Diana said, "was the week before, he changed his insurance policy. He crossed me off as beneficiary. It was a trivial sum but it's the thought that counts. Remember that, Annabell."

"Then what happened?" Annabell stared at her.

"The state of California got the money. And I got the idea," Diana said. She smiled.

Annabell was looking into the windows of the boutiques. Diana remembered this time three years ago. It was early in her sobriety, when the stories she heard struck her like so many blue rocks, when she felt physically assaulted and permanently engraved by what she heard, the words and relevations.

Diana Barrington remembered one story perfectly. It was about a woman who tried to appear normal. So she continued to go to the gym, to her aerobic classes and AA meetings. She didn't tell anyone that she was drinking.

On New Year's Eve she went to the Morton Douglas Gallery party that she attended every year. She stood in a corner with her back to the wall. She wore her new holiday outfit, a black velvet gown heavy with gold beads in a mock bullet motif. She wore gold high heels and gold hooped earrings and three gold bracelets on her left arm. She was wearing Deneuve perfume. She was chain-smoking. She kept staring at the door, as if expecting someone. At eleven o'clock precisely, he walked in.

"You remembered," the woman said. She had mentioned the party to him. She had once showed him the invitation.

"What did you think? Yeah. I remembered." He stared at her.

He was wearing a three-piece black suit with a cream stripe. He was wearing a red Gucci tie. He had shaved. His hair was cut. The woman wanted to remember the shade of his hair, how it seemed equal parts brown and gray and red.

"You like my suit? You never saw me dressed up before. I do business in this. I look like a Beverly Hills lawyer, right?" He turned around in a small circle so she could admire his entire body. He looked like a westside attorney. No one at the gallery would think he was a heroin addict, bank robber, drug pilot, and assassin.

"I had to sneak in and out of Chicago for this suit," he explained. He touched her arm. "Kiss me."

"I've been drinking," the woman whispered.

"Me too." He smiled. He was humming. He looked as if he had red light bulbs in his eyes.

Then he was reaching for her. She leaned into him. She had developed the curious notion that she could not refuse him anything. They embraced and she could feel the gun tucked into the small of his back. He tasted of brandy and something like bitter lemon. The juxtaposition of the Gucci tie and the revolver made her breathless. That's what the woman said at the meeting, something about his suit jacket and the gun.

It began to rain. She could see the boulevard through the plate-glass gallery windows. The leaves looked like moist tropical stars. There was a sudden sense of green. It was a sexual green, assaulting the boundaries. It contained a sense of delinquency. It was a green that promised more than intimacy or even outrage. A green that could shock you. And the boulevard sounded like a river.

"I got a boat at the Marina," he said, as if telepathically. He knew she thought of the fluid realms. He extended his arm to her. She wanted to memorize his hand. She knew it wouldn't always be there.

She was staring at his hand, the thick gold ring. "Come on," he said. "I got a yacht. Five minutes from here. Guy owes me a favor. He's out of town. I got the keys. You'll like it. I can tell. And I got us some party items. For our private New Year's Eve party." Then he told her, exactly, what these party items were. He whispered in her ear.

"You know, the tooth fairy shined me on last night," Annabell said.

"What are you talking about?" Diana demanded. She stopped walking. She was out of breath.

They were standing in front of another clothing boutique. Everything on display was black. There were black leather miniskirts and black leather jackets with and without fringe and studs. There were black feathers in black hats and black veils falling from black velvet brims. There were black feather boas.

"The tooth fairy," Annabell was saying. "Here I am, practically eight. It's only my third lost tooth and guess what? No tooth fairy for Annabell." Her daughter put her hands on her hips.

"I'm sorry," Diana Barrington said. She was still thinking about the woman and the bank robber. She can remember the details. There was a Jacuzzi on the yacht. He switched on a tape. There were speakers everywhere. It was Bob Seger's "Hollywood Nights." He knew the words. They sang together. It was raining. He was holding a champagne glass. He was naked. He was standing in the water dancing. The wide gold chains around his neck were bouncing against his flesh. She kept thinking that she had never before loved a man who wore gold chains. His gun was resting on top of his suit jacket.

Diana Barrington became aware of a disturbance near her. It was Annabell. Her daughter had stopped walking. Annabell stared at her, sullenly.

"Maybe the tooth fairy can come back tonight," Diana offered.

"Oh, I don't think so," Annabell decided. "It's too late. And I hate my life."

"Do you mean that?" Diana suddenly wanted to light a cigarette. But she no longer smoked.

Annabell thought about it. "No," she said, after a moment.

"Why do you say these cruel things?" Diana wanted to know.

"Just teasing," Annabell replied.

It was evening on Melrose Boulevard. A red glare was rising from within the boutiques. The red bulbs had been switched on. They etched pathways in the darkness, a hint of heat and corruption, of something profoundly tarnished.

"I hate being teased," Diana recognized. "Will you stop?"

"Okay." Annabell sounded accommodating.

Diana pressed her daughter against her chest. She kissed her and smelled her hair. Annabell's hair smelled of wind and salt and soap and wood. It was cool against her lips.

The night was rising. The lights were brighter, everything seemed painted with the colors of neon, pinks and purples that appeared irradiated. They passed a shop where poinsettia plants had been arranged to resemble an enormous Christmas tree. The night was entering the blue register. It was about to turn a serious shade of cobalt, pronged and cold. There was nothing innocent about it. It occurred to her that this was the sort of blue that inspired the invention of electricity. It was the blue of what you don't want to meet in the dark.

Diana remembered the last time she saw Carlotta McKay. It was nearly a year ago. It was a few days before Christmas. They met at the West Beach Café. They wore suits and sipped their tea. They were dipping their scones into whipped cream.

"I have a surprise for you," Carlotta McKay was saying.

Diana smiled. She assumed Carlotta was giving her the jade and diamond earrings that she had admired for the past twenty years, the ones she was continually borrowing. Or perhaps Carlotta was giving her the diamond bracelet with the ruby clasp she had inherited from her great-grandmother. Diana Barrington would take the appropriately wrapped box from Carlotta's hand. She prepared herself to appear amazed and grateful. She covered another pastry with whipped cream.

"I'm going in for surgery," Carlotta said. "And you're not invited."

Diana felt wide-awake. "What are you talking about?"

"I'm talking about recurrence. I'm talking about a biopsy. And how you won't be there." Carlotta patted the side of her mouth with the lilac linen napkin.

"Of course I will. I'll drive you, check you in, bring flowers." Diana felt sick. "I'll buy you a new bathrobe."

"I don't want you, dear," Carlotta said. "I don't want you surreptitiously measuring my tubes and counting stitches. You're always taking invisible notes. I know how disappointed you must be. You've been preparing for this inevitability for years. What an irony."

"What you are saying?" Diana was staring at her.

"We must sever our destinies," Carlotta said. She stood up. She was wearing a red Chanel suit with black shoes and a black silk scarf. "Don't look like that. After all, I might not even die. I might just continue with more bad men and marginal arrangements."

"We've had bad luck," Diana tried. "Your cancer."

"Your nervous breakdown," Carlotta said.

"I was psychotic for months," Diana remembered.

"Fifty-nine days," Carlotta corrected. "I counted."

"You actually counted?" Diana is surprised.

"Anyone else, I would have called the paramedics."

"Was I that bad?" Diana wanted to know this.

"I had to lead you by the hand," Carlotta said.

"You know I love you. You are the only human being besides may daughter that I have ever loved," Diana admitted. "You are my best friend."

"And that was something," Carlotta offered. Was, in the past tense.

"But we're blood sisters," Diana remembered.

"I have to go," Carlotta said. "You're becoming maudlin."

Carlotta left the restaurant. She was in the parking lot. Diana Barrington followed her. She wanted to run after her, to sit in her lap, perhaps.

"I can't live without you," Diana realized, suddenly, brokenly.

"It's time for you to learn," Carlotta McKay said. She snapped the lock on the door of her black Jaguar. Then she drove away.

"You're doing it again," Annabell observed.

"Talking to myself?" Diana Barrington asked.

They were almost at the studio where Annabell had her violin lesson. Christmas trees were positioned in the windows of the stores. There were wreaths and strings of lights. But the decorations seemed surprisingly subdued. She had expected something more dazzling. It occurred to her that the absence of tinsel might be a side effect of the plague.

"You nod your head. You smile. You frown. You move your hands." Annabell demonstrated. "It's like you're leading an orchestra."

"I'm just blocking in some memories," Diana explained. "I'm saying good-bye."

"Oh," Annabell said, after a moment. It was a small round sound, a kind of illumination. Diana felt it was visible in the dark, that it lingered, that it had a heat and a morphology. It was an unfinished thing, waiting.

Of course the darkness was filled with unfinished waiting things, Diana Barrington was thinking. She had considered these facts of the darkness during Annabell's lesson and again when they were driving. Sunset Boulevard was a series of chateaus and villas outlined and embossed with lights. Each separate tree was delineated. It was garish but not entirely unpleasant.

"I'm going to be forty-one," Diana Barrington announced.

"I'm going to be eight," Annabell Barrington reminded her.

"Forty-one is far more significant."

"Not to me," Annabell stood her ground. "To me, eight is everything."

"What does eight mean, precisely?" Diana was interested.

"I can read, so I'm never lonely. You told me that, remember? A child who can read is never lonely. I can do math. I can spell. I can write my own stories. I may start a novel soon. And I'm more mature now. I'm much more sophisticated. I understand patterns. And I have a fabulous attention span," Annabell said.

"You said the same thing last year," Diana pointed out.

"But this year I'm in love," Annabell told her.

"With the boy from art class? The one who drew the raccoons? Sean?"

"Yes," Annabell said. She closed her eyes and smiled.

Diana Barrington attempted to evaluate this. They were driving home in the dark. She must remember to put a dollar underneath Annabell's pillow. She must remember the tooth fairy. As she parked the car, she noticed the orange trees near the curb. All the orange trees were heavy with fruit. They seemed an odd juxtaposition in the chill. A car passed. In the headlights, she glimpsed a sudden island of bird of paradise, their orange heads prehistoric and shy, loitering in the dark.

It was cold on the Friday evening of *Fiesta de las Luces*. The children had to wear red, and Diana Barrington had purchased a new red velvet dress specifically for this presentation of "Jingle Bells." Annabell was extremely pale. Her fingers clenched. She kept looking in the mirror.

"I can't go through with this," Annabell said.

"Of course you can. Don't be silly," Diana managed.

"I'm the worst," Annabell suddenly concluded. "I'm so horrid I throw everyone else off. My violin playing really sucks."

"You're not that bad. And you're only responsible for yourself," Diana pointed out, pleased with how well she discerned and expressed these principles. I am learning how to mother, Diana realized. I am distilling entire moral universes into single lines. She is awed with herself.

They were driving to Annabell's school. There were lights like a string of stars in the trees. White lights lined the balconies of Spanish mansions, the turrets and arches. White lights and silver lights wound through the low bushes beside driveways. White lights rose vertically up the trunk of a tall palm. White lights lay along the electric gates and fell across trees like a downpour of crystal. White light was reflected back in massive arched windows. Red and green Christmas lights were extinct. It was white or silver now, elegant and cold. The separate branches of trees were outlined. No one on Mulholland seemed to be obsessed with the plague.

"Are you going to cry?" Annabell wanted to know.

"Why would I cry?" Diana glanced at her daughter.

"You cry every year. You say *Fiesta de las Luces* breaks your heart," Annabell reminded her.

It is the resonances rather than the production values, Diana thought as she parked the car. The way our children stand before us, with wings, with ceremonial robes, reciting from Genesis. They bow. We applaud. The earth is renewed. That was what she was thinking as she took Annabell to a backstage area. Her daughter was immediately embraced by other little girls in new red dresses. There were violin cases on a table. "Is Sean here yet?" Annabell asked, hands on her hips. "Where's Sean?" She was gone without a backward glance.

Diana drove to a florist. She bought roses and had them wrapped with red ribbon. Then she sat in the school auditorium. She was early. She was trying to synthesize the meaning of forty-one in case Annabell or anyone asked. She senses that she can do this. There is something sitting at the radiant blue edges. Yes. She can go in and touch it.

I am forty years old, she thinks. This is what I know. There is always too much ocean, too much blue and green. We are partial and haunted. We have small hands. We applaud our mediocrity. We will celebrate anything.

This is life, this fragility between wintery places punctuated by the heartbreak of jungle green which is a form of tenderness that perhaps whispers your name once as it passes.

This is what Diana Barrington is thinking as *Fiesta de las Luces* begins. What is there, really? The harbor? The orchids? The canvas for painting and sails? The almost-eight-year-old daughter you name for bells in December, this

Annabell? A love affair, a depot, a seaside hotel. A few post-cards and it's done.

On stage, children are dressed as shepherds. There is a skit about Mary and Joseph and the dangers of leaving home without the American Express card. Eventually the second-grade violin and cello section begins to play. It is perhaps the single worst rendition of any song that anyone has ever heard. It is so aggressively terrible that the audience laughs with embarrassment. There is a sense of shock. Then the audience erupts with wild spontaneous applause.

Annabell is staring into the darkened auditorium, methodically searching for her with wide and intense eyes. Annabell is the palest child on stage. She seems confused by the magnitude and enthusiasm of the applause. The conductor has the violin and cellos take a bow. Then he has them play it a second time.

Diana does not take her eyes off her daughter, the trembling Annabell who is playing "Jingle Bells" again. It occurs to Diana Barrington that it is all a matter of ruins and the improbable communications of the dead to the dead that rise in a waste of midnights. Our children wear velvet robes and offer ritual dialogue. This is how history talks. This is the dialect of centuries.

Annabell takes another bow. The violins and cellos disappear. Later, Annabell returns with stapled-on wings as a member of a chorus. She sings in a language Diana cannot place.

This is why we consecrate the days, Diana Barrington is thinking. Our birthdays and festivals, our rites and gods, these are the notes in the void. This is sacred, the invisible bones of hours and situations, infected with emotion.

Here are the bells you never forget, the plaza, the lips, the way rain on a boulevard in December once seemed the green of a jungle river in Asia, in a region you have never actually seen. The way the boulevard seemed to steam. You can see it out a plate-glass window. It is these impossible intimacies. We call this relevation. And isn't it a form of grace? The shed selves, these shells we leave in the air, these configurations we have touched and discarded, these former and partial versions, these earlier drafts, these sudden mutations and inspired morphologies? And the hands and mouths we memorize.

In the darkness are collections of holy seconds. How you saw him on the boulevard and the way he turned when his name was called, as if in that brief stasis, in that sudden autumn silence, came the resolution of the elements at last recognizing themselves.

Always the curtain is closing. We know what this means. We are almost forty-one after all, and certain behaviors have accrued of their own accord. We see the curtain close and we stand. We applaud. Our children wear ceremonial garments, velvet and wings. They stand motionless before us. We present them with bouquets.

"But it didn't sound right," Annabell persists. "It was my fault."

"It wasn't your fault," Diana assures her.

"You're not crying," Annabell notices.

"That version of the nativity may have brought me to my senses," Diana says.

Annabell considers the permutations of this. They are walking toward the car. In the darkness are the carcasses of the abstractions, the cities we have not yet seen, the water that could be any green canal or river and the holy site any abandoned stone. Always there is a distance you cannot pacify, she is thinking. Always sunset lingers like silver across the aqueducts. You know what the lovers whisper.

"Why did everyone applaud so?" Annabell asks. She stops walking. She places her hands on her hips. Her wings flap lightly in the wind. Diana is carrying the violin case.

"They appreciated your effort," Diana says, after a pause.

Annabell seems satisfied. They are walking across the school parking lot. The wind is blowing. The sky is almost white with clouds. They are holding hands.

"You're not talking to yourself," Annabell observes. "Are you?"

"No."

"Was that true about your father? Killing himself?" Annabell asks.

"What do you think?" Diana wants to know this.

"No way. Your father would never be so mean," Annabell tells her. "Would he?"

"Of course not," Diana agrees quickly.

"I knew it," Annabell says. She skips lightly along the path. "I knew you were just kidding."

They walk in the darkness. Suddenly Annabell says, "What are you looking at?"

"The lie of night," Diana replies. "The truth of night."

"Where is it?" Annabell is staring at her, into her.

Diana points. Annabell follows the line of her arm. "By the trash can? Or the tree?" Annabell asks.

Diana considers her options. "A bit to the left of the tree," she says finally.

Annabell is staring at the dark as if her life depended on it. "Yes," she says with excitement. "I can see it."

"You can?" Diana does not smile. "You are one exceptional child, Annabell," she says, after a moment.

Diana Barrington is thinking if they hold hands they can see in the darkness without their eyes. There is no darkness.

It is all inhabited. It is dense with what has been cast off and barely survived, the events that also have half-lives. And the buildings, the inventions, the plazas and kisses. These are the bones of the known and the mysterious, all of the blue things racked by moon. This is what glistens in the dark, the underbelly where we have lit matches and blown out candles and intoned wishes. It is in these clairvoyant ruins where we live between improvisations, consecrating the moments with our prayers and lies. Always we are abandoning the journey of recognizable destinations, the harbor with the breakwater and buoys. It is in the ruins of this darkness that we absolve the ones who love us badly. In the darkness where we know ourselves absolutely and we are fueled by ancient griefs and luminous without stars.

ABOUT THE AUTHOR

KATE BRAVERMAN lives in Los Angeles. She is the author of four books of poetry and the novels *Lithium for Medea* and *Palm Latitudes*. *Squandering the Blue* is her first collection of short stories.

3 9507 00002 4439

WITHDRAWN

WITHDRAWN

Braverman, Kate.
Squandering the blue, stories.

WITHDRAWN